Masquerade

Masquerade

short fiction

E<small>DWARD</small> L<small>EWIS</small>

Red Hen Press

2006

Masquerade
Copyright © 2006 by Edward Lewis

Cover art by Joan Lewis
Book and cover design by Mark E. Cull

ISBN 1-59709-064-6
Library of Congress Catalog Card Number: 2005937042

Red Hen Press
www.redhen.org

The City of Los Angeles Cultural Affairs Department, California Arts
Council, Los Angeles County Arts Commission and National Endowment
for the Arts partially support Red Hen Press.

First Edition

For Millie,
who shines the light.

Contents

Introduction

Ed Lewis writes a world that transcends war, peace and the strange combined turbulence of racism, poverty and madness that makes up America in the 21st century. With deft strokes he gives us characters that haunt us like black and white photos: Jet-setters, troubled teenagers, Vietnam Vets, migrant workers, and ordinary people. His stories are inhabited by the Americans of Zinn's *A People's History of the United States*. One wonders how a Hollywood producer dipped his fingers in the unearthly fissuring fabric of the American everyman. Lewis gives us union workers, Cesar Chavez, the migrant labor movement in California with startling color: "The color in front of me changed, first to chartreuse then abruptly to a bright orange. I looked up. The line of trucks outside Campbell's Tomato Soup plant went on as far as I could see. Crushed tomatoes covered everything. The bright orange began to mix with the dull, dark red liquid that flowed from the tomatoes. It smelled like blood" (33).

The stories remind one of Harold Pinter, the world is always slightly off kilter. The fabric is full of desire, secrets. Secrets clearly fascinate this author. One of the most haunting stories is of a Colonel who marries a Vietnamese woman his father, a general, refuses to acknowledge. After his father's death, he shows his wife a letter written in 1969 describing the atrocities of the war including the events of Mai Lai.

His wife Sung Hee cannot touch him in his grief. He is out of reach. In the end, the splintered fragments of the American psyche are what we are left with and a grief we are not equipped to process. A man who has returned from war, finds his father living among crazed racist killers, and attempts in thought particles to sort it out: "Maybe it was Post something-or-other Syndrome the intern told him he had. Christ knows there was plenty to cry about, but he hadn't shed one tear the whole time there. It wasn't that he never cried—he was always self conscious about the way he teared up at the movies—but there was a good reason he couldn't in Vietnam. The women, the old men, the children, they never cried when their villages were littered with corpses, never called out in pain, even after a grenade tore a limb off their bodies. Not ever, when one of us could see or hear them" (101).

Ed Lewis has created a collection of American stories that reflect the landscape of distinct cultures and the underbelly of a troubled psyche. America has not come to terms with our history, diversity, languages, or the two hundred years (fast growth for a country). Some of the stories point to unbearable longing, some to chasms between class and race. Others like light moving across the trunk of a tree in a dark forest, move toward the possibility of humanity rising above itself. America has yet to grow up. We have emerged a stark, starving demanding adolescent who doesn't know who they are or what they want, just that we do want and that we remain uncomfortable in our skin.

—Kate Gale
President, PEN USA

Masquerade

Bottomless Well

In New York City, in any big city for that matter, a man lying in the gutter is as noteworthy as a car cruising by; that he was a soldier made as much difference to the passersby as it would if the car were a Chevy or a Ford.

It took a while for Private First Class Jeffrey Williams to realize what had happened. He remembered standing on the sidewalk outside the building Margo worked in, unsure about going in. How many times had he wished he'd listened to her that day?

How long ago was it? A year? Two? A lifetime?

He never saw the half-ton hit a pot hole and drop a load of pipe onto the street, what he heard was a mortar shell exploding, and he dived to the ground, covering his head to protect against shrapnel.

An Indian who looked old enough to have fought Custer helped him to his feet. He said something about a bottomless well staring at the sky, but before the soldier could ask him what the hell that was supposed to mean, he disappeared. The Cong were like that.

Williams checked his inside pocket, the roll of film was still there. It was Friday the thirteenth; his watch said four-thirty. He wasn't about to let her see him looking like a bum, which meant he had the weekend to shape up before he tried again.

He needed to find someplace where he could curl up and go to sleep and hope that when he got up he'd find it was all just a bad dream. Central Park was only a block or so away; maybe he'd find an empty bench or a quiet spot under a tree.

The park was filled with people, joggers puffing like steam engines pulling a line of freight cars up a steep grade, kids on roller skates, couples just strolling, lovers who saw no one but themselves. A pair of squirrels running around a tree in a mating chase reminded him it was spring. A mocking bird was staking out his territory, and Williams looked up to see if he could spot the little master of many voices. It was that time of the month when you could see both the sun setting and the moon rising, when even the heavens seemed indecisive, like things could go one way or another. Maybe that bottomless well held the answer.

There weren't any vacant benches, and a construction crew that seemed to be drilling for oil (why not, they had derricks in the middle of L.A.), made searching for quiet hopeless. He'd have to find a room someplace. Downtown would be the direction to head in, out of the high rent district, just so long as he didn't pass by Margo's office again.

A cart selling hog dogs on Seventh Avenue was just getting ready to move on.

In Junior High it showed up every day at lunch time. When he scrimped enough change from his weekly allowance, he'd dump the lunch his mother made and indulge in a spicy dog smeared with mustard.

He bought a chili dog and a root beer, and carried them over to a low cement wall that bordered a nearby church, the only place in sight where you could sit down. People taking a break from the hectic pace of the city didn't seem to be enjoying their leisure moment, like they were doing something forbidden and were afraid of being caught. He knew that feeling well. The army instilled a strong dose of intimidation.

The man he sat down next to glared at the mud-splattered uniform. "You can't beat a rag-tag army in Vietnam, the least you can do is have enough pride in your uniform to keep it clean."

It certainly wasn't intentional that in turning to him the root beer poured onto the man's suit. A hard right to the jaw toppled Williams off the ledge. The maxim drummed into the male American psyche, if you're hit, hit back, hadn't taken with Williams. He just watched as the bully strode away.

A very tall black man lifted him to his feet.

"On furlough, private?"

"Discharged. Couple days ago."

"The uniform's not too popular right now. You could trade it in for some civvies at the Salvation Army. There's one down a ways on Sixth Avenue."

Christmas time outside Wanamakers Department Store in downtown Philly, pilgrim-costumed men and women rattling tambourines over a kettle. His mother always made sure to make a contribution, but she never put the money into the pot herself. She gave it to her son to do, no doubt thinking it might make a better person of him.

The volunteers who called themselves soldiers never stopped pitching the product that sustained their enterprise, the salvation of souls. At this particular time in Private Williams' life he didn't figure he had one, so he nodded agreeably at whatever they preached. The second hand brown worsted suit they gave him hung on his frame like a hand me down from a better fed relative. He was glad to get rid of the khaki, he'd never seem himself as a soldier, but the uniform had at least defined who he was and what was expected of him.

Harold Lloyd hanging on for dear life forty stories above the street, people rooting for him to fall off.

A liquor store a few doors down beckoned him like a half-clothed woman. 'Just one pint can't hurt,' he thought and was about to walk in when a man coming out of the deli next door caught his eye. The cab parked at the curb identified him. A New York fifty, which meant he'd seen everything a hundred times over and could answer any question if he wanted to, he usually had no time for talk other than to ask a fare 'where to.' He had a few bites left on his Danish, and was in an uncharacteristically gracious mood. "Nice day."

Williams nodded and asked if he knew a halfway decent place a person could stay for a night or two without breaking the bank.

"The "Y" on thirtieth is closed . . . trying to get rid of cockroaches, which is like dreaming this month's payment on the car is your last. Try the Chelsea . . . Twenty-third and Eighth. She's like a faded beauty contestant down on her luck, and like any old broad in that neighborhood, she comes cheap." Pleased with his imagery, he even offered a cheery, "Good luck."

Williams defied temptation and passed the liquor store without going in, but he knew the difference between a skirmish and a war.

It was run down now, but the Chelsea Hotel was once frequented by artists and writers, its past providing a veneer that elevated it above the city's other relics. Faded photographs of old time movie stars lined the walls of the lobby, buzzing now with a crowd celebrating the start of a weekend, young hip wannabes and for real actors, models, and assorted fringe players who favored the bar in the basement over the in-spots of the Village. It was too small to contain them all, but that was part of its appeal. They carried their drinks like designer purses, and milled around as though looking for someone in particular, which was rarely the case.

Marijuana smoke, one more hurdle in the steeplechase Williams was running, masked the smell of mildew that would return defiantly as soon as the bar closed. The army never acknowledged that it made drugs available to camouflage the danger and miserable conditions it placed its troops in, but if they had, he knew he'd be one of the statistics, living on the border of addiction.

The desk clerk, someone you'd remember even after a brief encounter, looked a little like what would happen if someone putting together a display dummy on Fifth Avenue mismatched the head and body. He had the build of an athlete, not one of the grotesques that played guard or tackle, more like a sixty yard dash man or maybe a tennis pro, but the head was of a completely different mold, delicate features, soft eyes that watered a lot, an almost feminine mouth.

He gave the soldier the choice of a room with a view of Twenty-third Street, or one facing the brick wall two feet from the building next door, with or without a bath.

"Barrymore slept in the hotel."

"Which one?" Williams asked.

He shrugged:

"Just Barrymore."

He pointed to an enlarged photograph behind the desk:

"Gloria Swanson too. Know who she was married to?"

"Wallace Beery."

The clerk raised his eyebrows:

"Not many people know that."

"I was a film major in college. Look I've had a rough day, Wallace Beery was never one of my favorites, I don't care what I look out on, and I've forgotten what a private bath looks like."

It probably got him the worst room in the place, but he didn't bother to look around at what was really an overblown closet. He got right into what was meant to pass for a bed. For the first time in god knows how long, there were no bad dreams.

He might have slept all through the next day, but the sound of water striking the window awakened him with a start. Rain muffled footsteps, and it didn't take long to learn you better be wide awake unless you wanted to trade a body bag for a chance you might survive another miserable day in the jungle.

It used to always be a treat. Rainbows, unplanned double features, the house cooling off in the summer, sniffles from a wet head or wet feet that meant a few days of pampered bed care.

He looked out the window. A rushing waterfall was so close he could reach out and touch it, the brick wall of the building next door providing a slicker surface than Niagara Falls. He pulled up a chair and fell under the hypnotic spell of endless water moving effortlessly as if it were riding a toboggan or an ice sled.

His bladder brought him back to reality. The pay phone just outside the john at the end of the hall reminded him he ought to call the coast. The Morris Agency had promised to hold his job until he got out. Just the thought tensed him up, not the way combat did but still unpleasant. He didn't look forward to being in the Hollywood jungle again, never knowing which arm that was patting you on the back held the knife that could destroy your career. In 'Nam's jungle the enemy was Death, but it was so outrageous to contemplate, it was kept almost completely submerged. When you saw it happen to others there was relief it wasn't you, then the image was consigned to the repository of nightmares.

It was still raining but he was edgy as hell and had to get out. 'Should have picked up an umbrella at that Salvation joint,' he said, talking to himself. The man in the elevator with him said there were street vendors all over town that sold umbrellas for a buck.

"They only come out when it rains. Like worms."

He didn't mind getting wet, that happened almost every day in 'Nam, but he worried about his suit. It wasn't like he had something to change into, and he needed to be careful with his money, the army's disability checks wouldn't resemble a living wage. With the skill most New Yorkers perfect even before they wear long pants or short skirts, he dodged under assorted canopies and overhangs, and made his way to a coffee shop a block away.

He didn't really feel like eating, but he had to keep from getting hungry later when the price of even the lowliest sandwich went up, as though what you did at night was a special privilege you had to pay a premium for. He never did understand why matinees were cheaper, the same people doing the same thing, in this case the same chow.

Half way through a greasy hamburger, a wave of nausea began insisting he give it back. That would have meant pissing away half a buck so he fought it off, wrapped the rest of the burger in a paper napkin, and put it in his pocket.

He needed something to do, a place to kill time.

Someone gave him the detective story for his birthday. It was about a private eye. His name might have been Archer. They were waiting for him in his apartment. He went into an all night movie house, one of the cheap ones that didn't run features, just shorts, cartoons and newsreels, and stayed in there half way through a day and night.

There was one just like it a few blocks from the restaurant. They called it a theater but it smelled more like a latrine. After an hour or so Williams left.

The sun was shining! Buildings that two hours ago were a depressing gray, sparkled like newly scrubbed puppies. You could even see the cracks in sidewalks stripped of layers of dirt accumulated since the last downpour.

And the smell.

The first time they made love, just out of the shower, arms wrapped tight around one another, no perfume on her, just the smell of fresh water.

He was curious about all the sights he'd heard about but never seen. Times Square seemed like a good place to start. He skirted around the seedy parts of 42nd Street, aiming to see the good, he'd had enough of the other. Posters in the theater district reminded him he was hopelessly out of touch, the only familiar name was Lauren Bacall in something called 'Applause.' He always liked her but by the time the show came to LA, if it ever did, it was more likely than not that a pinch hitter would be taking her place.

Billboards that hovered over the Square dwarfed the living things below, John Wayne a dozen times bigger than life in something called 'True Grit,' George C. Scott just as tall, standing in front of a gigantic American flag, jaw jutting out like Mussolini's and looking every inch the General he was glorifying.

The record store he was standing in front of was playing top 20 songs, none even faintly familiar. The current number one hit came on, it was pretty catchy. 'Raindrops falling . . .' perfect background music if only this was a movie and he was playing the lead. A flyer in the window caught his eye, Duke Ellington was giving a concert of sacred music at Saint-Sulfice Church in Harlem. Weird. He never associated God with jazz, but he figured if you were a believer you could connect the big 'G' to anything, lots of people seemed to.

The ticker tape of lights that circled the Triangle Building reported that Apollo 13 was launched successfully from Cape Kennedy, which interested him not at all, same with the riots going on in an upstate New York penitentiary no one ever heard of except for the cons and their families.

He was getting tired and headed back to the hotel. It was a long walk and when he finally got there he figured he was entitled to a nightcap. He'd been to a few bars but none like the one downstairs, no chairs or tables, no waiters, just a counter where you picked up your own drink, and standing room if you were lucky. He felt totally out of place, like he was at a party where he didn't know anyone. The second hand suit didn't help matters.

People were elbow to elbow, and the close contact suddenly panicked him. He needed to get out of there fast, and almost knocked down a woman blocking his exit.

He was sweating, and could only mumble, "I'm not feeling well. Sorry . . ."

"It's okay. I'm a little claustro myself."

He took a deep breath. "I'll buy you a drink."

She smiled at him. "Some other time."

On the way to his room, he thought about a Barrymore having slept in the hotel. If it was John they probably had to carry him up and undress him. He hoped it was John.

He was still wound up tighter than a busted yo-yo and took one of the sleeping pills they gave him when they let him out of the hospital. The army doctor told him he had an addictive personality but they gave him shit that was habit forming anyway. Nobody gave a damn. He thought about how they all said he was suffering from Post Traumatic Stress Syndrome, but the government wouldn't acknowledge the condition existed. Let the poor schmucks like him think what bothered them was all their own doing.

Well fuck them! He dumped the pills out the window, sorry it wasn't raining so they could be washed down proper. For a moment he was proud of himself, just for a moment. He needed those pills for Christ's sake! First thing in the morning he'd have to find the nearest VA hospital, and get the prescription refilled.

The drug kicked in fast and things were peaceful, until the dream.

'Get over to Company C, double time.'

He couldn't say for sure who was giving the order.

'Take all your cameras.'

The road is deserted, there are no sounds. It's a bad sign. He doesn't know what to do, and calls home on the walkie talkie.

'Call and have them pick you up,' his father tells him.

'I don't have their phone number.'

He heads for home. It's raining cats and dogs. His father lets him in the house.

'I can't find the place.'

'I have my own troubles,' his father replies, and takes him into the bathroom.

A woman is inside the toilet. Feces are floating all around her. She looks like his mother but she's Vietnamese. When she sees him she covers the bowl with a towel:

'Help me.'

He woke up groggy and confused, like he'd gotten a whiff of that poison the army sprayed all over the countryside. The pills always left him depressed. He wondered what people would be saying about him if he died, and tried to imagine his own funeral. Who would be crying? His mother and father probably, even though he didn't see much of them after he moved to the coast. Margo? Maybe. He was sorry he never sent the letter he wrote to her from Vietnam.

'I'm a combat photographer, the pictures I take are sent back to prove we're winning the war, pictures as phony as a politician's resume, posing every enemy corpse half a dozen times to inflate the body count, even assuming they were Cong, not civilians. You can get used to anything, like getting a whiff of ether or a shot of Novocain. I tried to make believe it was just a game. 'Smile you're on Candid Camera.' I hated myself for saying that to a kid who would never get to take his first shave.'

There was no point mailing it, the censors would black out every word, and he couldn't write anything really personal, not even that he missed her or that he was carrying her picture, the one he took on the ocean walk in Santa Monica under the big palm tree. Not the way things were left after the notice came from the draft board.

"Don't go."

"What are you talking about?"

"I'm talking about not taking part in a war that is immoral . . . unjust . . . and illegal to boot."

"So I fight Washington instead of Vietcong, right?"

"You don't fight anybody. You just don't become part of it."

"And how do you propose I do that?"

"Go to Canada. I'll go with you. We'll find a place together just like we were planning to do here."

"I'd be a fugitive the rest of my life."

"We can't predict the rest of our lives, but we can control what we do now."

"I don't want to be branded a traitor and a coward."

"People who know you and love you will never believe that. Taking a stand against something that's wrong is the act of a patriot. And a brave man."

"You're always so goddamn sure you're right. I'm not. I hope you'll wait for me."

"That's a line from a 'B' movie. I can't tell you how I'll feel about you when you come back a hero."

Splashing cold water on his face, trying to wash away the memories that plagued him, he caught a glimpse of himself in the mirror. His shoulders were stooped like an old man's, his face gaunt and lined, the eyes lifeless. He wondered if everyone had to confront his own ghost sometime in his lifetime.

At the VA hospital everything moved in slow motion, you took a number, sat down, and waited. He tried to think of something pleasant, but thoughts like that were as elusive as the fleeting glance he sometimes got of a beautiful woman passing by on the street. Here there were only white-coated attendants pushing frail men in wheelchairs. The smell of Lysol and antiseptic brought back troubling memories of the Atlanta hospital they shipped him to from Vietnam.

The nurse set up the breakfast tray, then walked over to the window: 'Best view in the hospital of Turner Field. If you had your camera you could get some shots of Dizzy Dean. He's pitching to-day.'

He suddenly remembered the roll of film he'd shot and hidden in an empty toothpaste carton! The toilet kit was in the bathroom. He almost knocked the tray over in his hurry to get there, his hands shaking like he had Parkinson's. It was still there.

For the first time it really hit him. He'd taken something that belonged to the army, something they wouldn't want anyone to see. It wouldn't go easy on him if he got caught. He remembered that GI ordered to stand at attention and not move, outside and in the rain. He didn't know why the soldier was being punished, for sure a helluva lot less serious than what he'd done. The poor bastard couldn't stand the flies swarming around him, big black ones that got into his eyes and ears and up his nostrils, and he broke down crying. They carried him inside and dumped him on his bunk like a duffel bag filled with dirty clothes.

The hospital room had a television set suspended from the ceiling, but he almost never turned it on. So much had happened since he checked out of the real world, he was like a an alien from a different planet, too far out of touch to try to catch up. He needed a distraction now, and surfed the channels looking for something besides the cop and hospital shows that phoneyed up violence and pain, the sitcoms that did anything to get a cheap laugh.

A show called '60 Minutes' was on, a guy he didn't know describing what was coming up, like the movie trailers they taught him how to make. Right there on top of the screen it said 'Produced by Margo Gross.'

He couldn't believe it! He knew she'd go far.

It came to him right away! She had the clout, and would know what to do with the film. She'd be proud of him too, risking his neck the way he had.

His luck had finally turned. Maybe, just maybe it wasn't too late. Maybe they could start all over again.

He got paper and a pen from the nurse, and started to write.

'They made me a combat photographer, courtesy of film school. I wrote you about it once before but I was afraid you wouldn't want to hear from me. You were right saying I was hypersensitive about feeling rejected.

This one day, the Lieutenant who commanded the unit I was to photograph, was smoking a joint when I got there. Name's Calley, he said, with two L's. Bring plenty of film, we're going to take out a Cong village. Mai Lai, which means good fortune. He thought that was funny.'

His hand began to shake. No way she'd be able to read his writing unless he settled down. That gave him time to think He'd be getting out of the hospital in a few days, why not tell her in person?

He couldn't get to sleep that night, couldn't get that Vietnamese woman, old enough to be his own mother, out of his mind, staring at him with hatred while he took pictures of her being raped.

He remembered a trick an actor once told him he used when he had trouble sleeping. Put whatever's bugging you onto a stage, and drop the curtain. When you raise it again the stage is bare, and you can play any character in any scene you make up.

He was ready to try anything. *Jimmy Stewart fighting government corruption, filibusters the Senate. Popeye after he's swallowed a can of spinach, saves Olive Oil.* It felt pretty good, and brought back the time when he believed he'd someday win an Academy Award, Best Original Screenplay, by Jeff Williams.

He couldn't wait for the morning, and it turned out to be one of those days even Angelenos would admire. There was no doubt. It was going to be a great day!

One thing more he had to do. He opened his toilet kit and took out a tiny hand carved wooden bird, the only thing he'd brought back from the jungle. He added a sentence to the bottom of the letter he was bringing to Margo.

'This is the only thing that survived in a hut we burned to the ground. I figured it was a magical bird, so I kept it. It hasn't worked out for me, maybe it will for you.'

Heading uptown towards the RCA Building, he caught his reflection in a store window. He couldn't show up in the Salvation Army suit.

A 'Checks Cashed' sign beckoned him in to one of the clip joints that prey on undocumented workers. Twenty per cent, take it or leave it. Fuck you! At the bank, before they'd give him the money, he had to practically pledge allegiance to the flag. Across the street, Alexander's Department Store had a sale on men's clothing. The slacks and shirt didn't set him back too much, and he felt like the person he used to be.

The lobby of the building was so big you could launch a kite inside. Just scanning the directory boards was a daunting task. 'Sixty Minutes' occupied the eighty-first floor.

He'd been pretty cocky up until now, living out a day dream or two while he worked his way uptown, but now it was reality time. She might not even remember him! He put the roll of film in his hand for reassurance, decided maybe it was too early in the morning for someone in her position, and he sure didn't want to sit in an office and wait.

There was a coffee shop right off the lobby.

"Two eggs, scrambled. Coffee black and strong, please."

A rack of newspapers was by the door, the kind that had a long wooden pole holding each paper so it couldn't be lifted. There was one paper left. The moment he picked it up, the headline blind sided him.

'GOOD NEWS FOR LT. CALLEY. SENTENCE REDUCED.'

He was dreaming again! Another nightmare. A mistake, or another Calley, that could be it.

'Responding to the pleas of patriotic Americans, President Nixon reduced Calley's sentence from ten years in the Federal Penitentiary to nine months of house arrest.'

He could hardly breath, his hands shook.

'Calley will be permitted to accept speaking engagements. Sources who asked not to be named, say he'll be paid $10,000 an appearance.'

"Are you all right?" the waitress asked as she put the eggs and coffee down.

An alien. . . .

"Just a dizzy spell."

"My husband has them. Puts his head down and closes his eyes until it passes."

He stood on the sidewalk outside the building, like someone in a hypnotic trance. No one paid him any attention. He walked on. He was in the park. The benches were empty, it was quiet, the construction crew on a break or the job finished. A temporary barricade was around an open hole. It was easy to climb over.

He stared down, straining to see where it ended. Somewhere down there were all the really guilty ones, hidden, out of sight. Colonels, Generals, the Pentagon, the White House, everyone who knew the truth but didn't give a damn about anything but protecting the greedy spoils of their war.

He took the wooden bird out of his pocket, and stared at it. A Vietnamese man was carving it for his daughter. He looked up hoping to hear the sounds of a mocking bird again, but there were none. He stared at the sky until a bird appeared. He didn't know what kind it was but he marveled at how effortlessly it made its way across the sky. When it came closer he held up the wooden bird to see if they were similar. His was lifeless, only its past was still alive.

He dropped the bird into the hole, and listened for the sound that meant it had reached the bottom. It never came.

He stood motionless, staring down at the dark endless void.

He looked up at the sky. Not even a cloud whose ever changing form might hold some meaning. Nothing.

Someone approached, as silently as the Cong:

"Pure Colombian, special deal."

As automatic as saluting an officer, Williams reached into his pocket for the money.

He headed out of the park. It didn't matter in which direction.

Coyotes

The road winding up to Latigo Drive passed a dozen or so estates and finally dead ended at a California Ranch Style house. Modest by the standards of Bel Air, it sat on a promontory beyond which the ground fell off into a deep chasm.

The woman who answered the door was younger and a lot friendlier than I expected.

"I haven't done this before," she informed me. "Did they explain how it works?"

"They told me people in the area offer housing to film students from out of town. Rent free in return for some chores."

She nodded: "I'll show you the place."

She took my arm and led me on a path that circled behind the house.

"Don't expect too much. It was meant for a chauffeur, like Gloria Swanson's in Sunset Boulevard. My husband doesn't even want a house keeper around, so it hasn't been used."

We crossed a large flagstone patio; off to one side was a hot tub and a swimming pool. A little further on a cottage sat among a stand of eucalyptus trees.

"If it suits you the only thing you'd have to do is house sit when we're on location. My husband's a director. I'm an actress."

There wasn't much to see: one room, some basic furniture, a tiny bathroom in the back. It reminded me of the cabanas my parents used to rent on the beach in Atlantic City, just big enough if you wanted to lounge out of the sun or set up a table for lunch.

I mustered as much enthusiasm as I could: "It suits me fine."

"Good. There's some silly rule against it but I can put in a hotplate if you want."

I thanked her and she gave me the key.

By the time I moved in and unpacked it was late. I thought I'd kind of get my bearings, and went outside. The darkness was eerily quiet like someone with a remote control had pushed the mute button. I couldn't shake an uneasy feeling that moving here was a mistake.

Before going to sleep I looked under the bed. I started doing that around the time mother died. My father saw me one night and scolded me:

"The bible tells us to fear only god." He refers to the bible a lot.

This was the first time I'd done it since then.

I couldn't fall asleep. I needed to get my mind off wondering what was agitating me. I tried to remember my mother singing along with the musical teddybear she bought me when I was little. Some kids clutch blankets to feel safe, I slept with my teddy until it was restuffed and stitched so often it was no longer recognizable.

It was hard to remember her singing, most of the time she was sad. I used to think of different reasons why, like she didn't have the son she wanted, she hardly ever saw her parents after they moved to Arizona, she shouldn't have given up teaching. Sometimes I thought it was my father. He wasn't exactly affectionate, at least not that I saw.

Mother used to pick me up at school. After she died—I was in third grade—Joe, who drove the delivery truck, brought me to father's store. He was so tall he had to bend almost in half to get in and out of the car; muscles bulged all over him like the Hulk. I'd try to close my two hands around his arm—halfway was as far as I could get—he'd give the muscle a little tweak, my hands would bounce off like they'd been shot out of a cannon. My favorite thing to do while I waited for father to take me home was go upstairs to the spray room and watch Tony paint old furniture to look like new. I liked the smell of turpentine.

I began decorating my room with pictures of animals I cut out of magazines and newspapers. My father thought it was part of my thing with the teddybear but he was wrong. I just wouldn't tell him why I did it.

The second night in the cottage was as bad as the first; if it was going to go on like that I'd have to get some sleeping pills from the University Clinic. My father always told me if you can't sleep say a prayer and think of something pleasant. I skipped the prayer and thought about the time I won first prize, (five dollars), in a High School essay contest. It was when I decided to become a writer.

Everyone assumed I wrote the essay because Whitman died in Camden in a cottage on Mickle Street, not far from where we lived. 'A great writer, a great man,' is what I was always told, but what intrigued me were the quirky parts of the man, things skipped over like they weren't important and didn't matter. I was always drawn to the offbeat. He admitted to having six illegitimate children, but then you learn that he made that all up, which was pretty confusing until I found out he loved men, several of them actually. There was nothing wrong with that as far as I was concerned except he dressed and acted like a flamboyant rogue, what he wanted everyone to believe, when in fact the opposite was true; he was a very conservative man.

A month or so after I moved into the cottage, my landlady called. Her husband was going to shoot his new film in Vancouver, they were leaving Monday.

"It would be good if you moved into the house, the maid's room is never used. We're having a going away party Saturday night, so Sunday would be a good time." She was about to hang up but had an after thought: "Why don't you come? There will be lots of singles."

One of the first things I learned at film school, (not from faculty), was that without contacts forget it! I certainly didn't want to alienate my landlady, her husband being a director, and this might be a chance to meet people on the inside. Besides, she was being really nice.

The guests looked like they'd been provided by Central Casting: young, gym sculpted men who were waiters or actors or both, women who wore too much make-up, too little clothes, and perfume that seemed to have been bathed in. At the far end of the room one man, a generation older and a foot shorter than anyone else, was surrounded by a group of sycophants; I figured that was my landlady's husband. I couldn't get near him and wandered around trying to become part of a conversation, but the talk was all about agents they loved or hated, and parts they were up for or missed getting because the producer had a boyfriend or girlfriend. A starlet passing by called out cheerily: "The fun's like on the patio."

The insistent beat of Jimi Hendrix thundered out of speakers suspended from trees. A portable dance floor vibrated beneath writhing bodies that pantomimed sex acts rather than dancing. The hot tub held half a dozen bodies that were like corpses floating in the sea after a shipwreck, their eyes wide open, staring into the void. The women were naked, at least from the waist up. I didn't know if I could do that.

A man wearing a white tunic saw me staring at them, and approached. Less muscular than the others, he was the only person I'd seen at the party who wore glasses.

"LSD is taking them through that moment of twilight, that crack in the universe between daylight and dark. To quote Herman Hesse: 'they are in a magic theater, a world of pictures not reality, the only price of admission their mind.'"

"I can't imagine how it feels to be in a state of blissful tranquility."

"Infused with fluidity and the freedom to seek new paths. I haven't seen you around before. Actress?"

"A wannabe writer. At UCLA Film School."

He nodded approvingly: "There's a private screening Monday night you might find interesting." He took out a card and wrote down an address on the back: "If you decide to come I'll be outside at ten to eight. There's parking behind the building." He started to walk away, then turned back: "Not many women are but you wouldn't happen to be color blind by any chance."

"That's a weird question. The answer is no."

"Too bad. I'm doing research on hallucinogenic drugs. Vivid color perception is one of the constant…and I might add exciting effects it has. I'm curious about how it works on someone who doesn't see color."

The screening room was on Sunset Strip; the man in the white tunic was Dr. Harold Fulton, UCLA Associate Professor of Psychology, only now he wore black trousers, a black turtle-neck shirt, and a black scarf draped carefully around his neck. He wasn't about to get lost in any crowd. He said "Hello," told me I looked pretty, and ushered me into the room.

Four oversized lounge chairs were decorator coordinated with a fabric that covered the walls of the room. To one side was a small bar from which the dozen or so guests helped themselves to white wine. They seemed to be waiting the way you do for an elevator, only instead of glancing up to see which floor it's currently on they were focused on who might be coming in the door.

Several of them recognized the professor and made a point of letting him know that they did; like they thought they should or had to. While he circulated among them, my mind wandered back to something that at first seemed totally unconnected to the moment.

Often, on our way to Atlantic City, father would call on some of the tomato farmers in the area, customers of his. The store he inherited from my grandfather sold everything from clothing to furniture, all on the installment plan, which meant a little down, a little more every month. Twice a year the farmers would fill their trucks until they overflowed with the season's harvest, then line up for blocks outside Campbell's Tomato Soup plant in Camden, waiting for the weigh-in that would either mean food on the table or their kids would go hungry. While father spoke to the farmers, I'd play with the kids, mother would talk recipes in the kitchen with the wives. I thought about it now because although those families always came over to greet father when he drove up, they seemed uncomfortable, like they weren't sure why he was so friendly to them, and they had to be careful not to offend him. A lot like the way the professor was greeted.

The host arrived: Dennis Hopper. Notwithstanding the Chamber of Commerce propaganda, he was my first celebrity sighting. Needless to say, when the star greeted the professor before any of the other guests, I was pretty impressed.

One image summed the movie: Hopper and Peter Fonda cruising on revved up Harley-Davidsons down a deserted highway, nothing in the world mattering but whatever it was they decided to do. And nobody could stop them.

Everyone applauded when the credits came on at the end, and the professor proclaimed that Easy Rider would define a new American morality. He asked me for my opinion, in front of Hopper no less. I didn't think that romanticizing drugs and defying all rules of behavior was an ideal model, but of course I agreed. I'm a quick learner. I thanked the professor for the invite and at the door asked if he knew a lot of movie stars.

"Some. They're volunteers in the study I mentioned at the party."

"The color blind thing."

"I still haven't found a candidate that qualifies. You'd be a good subject, color blind or not."

I should have flat out said I wasn't interested, but things take on a different look in the glow that celebrity radiates, the way Vaseline spread over the lens of a camera flatters the subject.

"I can't do much of anything for a while. I'm house sitting starting to-morrow."

"Call me any time."

Before I left Jersey I'd sometimes browse through travel magazines and try to imagine what it would be like staying in one of those five star luxury resorts. I couldn't believe my luck, I had one now all to myself!

I didn't have a bathing suit, and it took me a while before I finally decided to strip down and dive into the pool stark naked. It was exciting in a way that surprised me, but I felt vulnerable and didn't stay in nearly as long as I could have. A stack of beach towels was near the pool, but instead of wrapping one around me, I stood in all my nakedness, staring out beyond the patio to where nature too was in its natural state. I felt free, free to dream, to do whatever I liked. The wind cooled my body, my arms were wrapped tightly around Dennis's waist, we sped down a deserted highway.

Eventide, moonless and starless, all that existed behind the house was a borderless black hole. I never believed there was nothing to fear but god, and looked under my bed again that night. A chilling sound startled me awake: it sounded like the pitiful whining of a child, but I knew it had to be something else. It went on and on, and when it turned into a frightening tangle of low pitched movements, I got goose bumps. Something horrible was happening. All I could think of were blind people being pushed, stumbling and falling.

As suddenly as it began, everything got unnaturally quiet. I felt shut up inside a closet, and tried to conjure up nighttime sounds that were familiar: street traffic, the siren of an ambulance, a plane overhead. Nothing. The silence was oppressive. I had to get out of bed, out of the room.

I went into the kitchen and warmed up a glass of milk, mother's antidote for restlessness. On the way back to my room I noticed a door I hadn't opened before. I wasn't in any hurry to get back to bed so I opened it. I was in a laundry room that held a washer and dryer and an extra refrigerator, its door covered completely with pictures. I turned on the light. Cutouts from dozens of photographs were arranged in a kind of collage. The photos were old, the girl in them only about ten, but I knew right away it was my landlady as a child. The pictures had all been taken on a farm, most of them with animals the girl clearly loved: a horse, a goat, a dog of mixed breed, a rabbit. I stared at the pictures, and tears came to my eyes.

The first time we stopped at her father's farm, Angelica showed me the decals she had pasted to the inside of a chest of drawers. They were all different kinds of animals, her secret world.

I saw the chest again in the paint shop. Tony was scraping the decals off. I told him I knew the girl who put them on and that it would make her sad if they were gone. He said: "It doesn't matter. She won't see this piece again."

I ran downstairs looking for my father. One of the salesmen told me he and Joe were on their way to repossess some furniture. I didn't know what repossess meant. He explained that if the payments didn't come in they took the furniture back.

My eyebrows scrunched together as I tried to understand. He misunderstood my concern and told me not to worry. I couldn't believe I heard him right when he said the boss always has a shotgun with him.

My father helped Joe unload a bed and a refrigerator from the truck. I asked him why he took things from people who are poor, things they needed. He quoted from the bible. "Merchants are princes, the honourable of the earth. To make a profit without another's loss is impossible." He said it was from Isiah Number twenty three.

I went back to my room and finally fell asleep, but at the price of a bad dream. I was in a morgue filled with endless rows of corpses. I walked up and down peering under the sheets, searching for someone. I didn't know who.

The next morning I had the kind of hangover nightmares leave you with. Everything depressed me: I shouldn't have left home; I didn't want to be like my mother, unhappy all the time; I didn't want to be alone in this empty house. I needed someone to talk to. I've heard it's not unusual when you're away from home for the first time, to keep everything that connects you with new people or places. The professor's card was in my wallet.

He asked me to meet him at a small restaurant on one of the trendy streets in Brentwood. It's no myth that girls mature quicker than boys, so my classmates weren't what you would call men, and there's a big difference between men and boys. Harold, he insisted I call him by his first name, was easy to talk to. Before long he knew all about the ghostly sounds and the morgue.

"You have an active imagination. I recently read a book about the ability of peyote to unleash the powers of creativity. It has particular application to writers whose challenge is to explore the unknown, to transform imagination into words. Give me your address, I'll send it to you.

The book was called The Teachings of Don Juan, a Yaqui Way of Knowledge. I found it pretty interesting for a while but then it got repetitive and boring. I waited a couple of days before I called him. You have to understand that I drink an occasional glass of wine, and I only tried pot a few times, so it wasn't for kicks or anything like that. I wanted his approval. I guess I wanted to be like those movie starts he knew. I told him I was ready to try the LSD, "Just once."

His house was in the Hollywood hills. The area is hard to describe, you really have to see it. Experience it would be more accurate. Imagine the era of silent movies: a Moorish castle, a Roman villa, a haunted house, a rock garden straight out of a fairy tale, all on one narrow, winding street. Harold's place was the Moorish castle. He was wearing a red velvet smoking jacket.

He gave me a tour of the house and told me it once belonged to Rudolph Valentino. I thought that was really neat. We ended up in a room with all the curtains drawn. The floor was covered with large pillows of varying shapes, all of them black; the only piece of furniture was the chair Harold sat in. A tape recorder was on the floor. He asked me to sit on the pillow next to it.

"Take off your shoes, make yourself comfortable."

I thought I'd be nervous, but instead I found myself caught up in an exotic make believe world: I was, after all, living in a cottage just like Gloria Swanson's chauffeur, she herself had surely been in this very room with Valentino, doing who knows what stars like that did in those days. I removed my shoes slowly and deliberately, took off my sweater, and arranged myself as seductively as I could on the pillow.

"I'm ready." For my close-up, I added to myself.

29

He handed me a cube of sugar:

"The acid is inside. Take small bites. It's important that you describe everything you see, all your thoughts, exactly how you feel."

I had an immediate desire to throw up. I was experiencing an unbearable thirst, and asked him to get me some water. He brought me a small glassful and said I couldn't drink but should just freshen my mouth with it. The water looked strangely shiny, glossy, like a thick syrup.

I was suddenly very confused. There was a clear thought in my mind but I couldn't speak. I wanted to comment on the strange quality of the water but what followed was not speech, it was the feeling of unvoiced thoughts coming out of my mouth in a sort of liquid form, an effortless sensation of vomiting without the contractions of the diaphragm, a pleasant flow of liquid words.

A supreme happiness filled my whole body. I reached out for a kind of yellow warmth that came from some indefinite place. I felt an irresistible impulse to jump, and did so with grace and mastery. The euphoria that possessed me was indescribable. I laughed until it was almost impossible to breathe.

The out of body experience was addictive, and without a second thought I agreed to another session. The evening it was scheduled for, my landlady unexpectedly returned.

"They're still shooting but I spotted a little and want to be close to my OB." She patted her belly: "Only three to go."

I hadn't even noticed that she was pregnant.

"You hardly show at all."

"That's sweet of you. I hate the way I look. Any problems?"

"It's been pretty quiet. A couple of nights there were some weird sounds out back."

"Oh the coyotes. They're very smart. Know what they do? The best actor in the pack sneaks out to the middle of the field and cries like a creature that's dying. Pretty soon some unsuspecting animal comes over looking for an easy meal. You can guess the rest."

I could, it gave me the creeps. I was glad I had something to look forward to that night.

"I'll pack up my things and move back to the cottage."

"No big rush. A few girlfriends are coming over tonight but they won't be here until eight or so. And oh, thanks for watching over things."

This time the LSD was baked into a round cake, a small one but larger than the cube of sugar. I'd find out why pretty soon.

I no longer lived in the real world. Things that had been ambiguous or unfathomable, beyond understanding, suddenly made sense, more than that, went beyond mere recognizability to a depth that couldn't be plumbed.

I saw my father standing in the middle of a field. The field vanished and the scene was the park I sometimes played in when I was little. My father and I were standing by an elm tree. I began to tell him things I could never say before, staggering things about my feelings toward him. He just listened and then was pulled or sucked away. I wept with remorse and sadness.

Something emerged from a strange star-like light on the tree, a shiny object that gave off an intense yellowish or amber light. The effect was startling. I reached out to touch it but suddenly became aware that a hand was on my thigh.

It was Harold. He had turned off the tape recorder and was nibbling on the cake. It was obvious what he had in mind.

He had intruded into my own private world, and I turned away angrily.

He said I was having a bad trip and should go into the bedroom and lie down. I wanted to be in my own bed. He drove me home but I wouldn't let him come into the cottage. He said I'd be all right in a little while and left.

As soon as the car pulled away I could hear music. It was one of the Beatles' tunes. I'd heard it a hundred times but I couldn't remember its name. The music was coming from the main house. I got out of bed like a sleepwalker.

For a while I stood at the edge of the property and stared down at the pitch black hole. I wanted to soar over it like a great bird, climbing higher and higher until I could touch the stars. The music changed. I didn't know the song, a haunting, caressing love song. I wanted to learn the words, I wanted to sing.

It was a warm night, the windows and doors to the house were open. I went inside. The women were taking turns snorting a line of coke. I recognized the starlet from the first party. She began to dance, alone but sensuously. I thought her beautiful.

In the middle of a refrain the music stopped. Quiet hung in the air like a heavy fog, every living thing seemed to be holding its breath. Then the pitiful whining started again, the tangle of low pitched movements.

Coyotes.

But the sounds were inside the house.

The room was jolted by sharp noises. They became louder, closing in on me like gigantic steps. Something, someone was coming towards me, silently, in slow motion. It was a man. One hand covered his face, the other held a knife aimed for my heart. I focused on the point of the blade, it gave off an intense yellowish or amber light. The effect was startling, exhilarating.

The color in front of me changed, first to chartreuse then abruptly to a bright orange. I looked up. The line of trucks outside Campbell's Tomato Soup plant went on as far as I could see. Crushed tomatoes covered everything. The bright orange began to mix with the dull, dark red liquid that flowed from the tomatoes. It smelled like blood.

Independence Day

1

Querida,

Manana empesamos a recoger la cosecha de fresas. To-
morrow we begin picking strawberries. I will have money to
send.

El nijo del granjero Sanchez esta aqui. El se queda en el
Rancho Los Cuevas. The son of the farmer Sanchez is here.
He stays at the Ranch of Caves. They sleep in holes cut into
the side of a hill. Like in a coffin.

Next week we vote whether to join a union. I am for it. El
Patro me veo. . . . The Patrone saw me talking to a reporter.
He wanted to know what I told her, and patted the pistol in
his belt. I will be careful.

Soon we will buy a small farm in Apodaca.

Mi amore, abrozos y besos para los chicos. Love, hugs and
kisses to the children.

Juan

2

Roberto, son of Juan and Maria Sanchez, brother of Jose, of
Elena, of Juanita and of the infant Cesar named in honor of
Cesar Chavez, is walking from Guadalupe outside of
Monterey, to Nuevo Laredo, a distance of two hundred and

fifty kilometers. From there he hopes to cross the border to Laredo, Texas, and make his way to California to find his father, last heard from six months ago. He is twelve years old.

He has with him an old road map that a trucker gave him as a tip for washing his windshield. It might have been a mean joke but for Roberto it is a precious possession, circled now with the route he will take: from Laredo, west along the border through Texas, New Mexico, and Arizona, to Riverside, California, the postmark on his father's last letter.

From Guadalupe to Vallecido, half way to Nuevo Laredo, dirt roads connect isolated farms that raise scrawny cattle and hogs. The only transportation is by horse or burro. Every twenty or thirty miles a roadhouse bar or general store with mostly empty shelves breaks the monotony of the arid moonscape. Occasionally there are small pools of muddy water maintained for the cattle that roam the fields searching for anything on which to graze. For Roberto the muddy pools are oases. He drinks what he can and fills the pottery flask his mother made him carry.

For food he depends on handouts from the impoverished farmers, scraps that he's careful to chew slowly. Sometimes an abandoned barn or storage shed provides shelter. Mostly he sleeps in the open fields, near some brush if he can find it. He knows about the mountain lions and the cougars, and keeps the knife his father made clutched in his hand. No one he meets asks where he is going.

Outside of Vallecido, a town of a few thousand, there is a dump, not the big city kind filled with garbage, (which would be a blessing), but where people get rid of things long broken and useless. You never know what you might find there, even something you could eat if you held your nose, so the strays in the area forage there, mangy dogs that are almost skeletons, desperate and mean.

There are six or seven of them, not counting the one the others drove away and who stands in the distance watching sadly. Roberto guesses it had a home of some sort not too long ago because there is still some flesh on the bones, but scars across its body tell of beatings. One foreleg is broken and it bends outwards like it's pointing accusingly at the man who abused him. Gray whiskers tell that he's suffered more than a few years.

Roberto sees what the dogs are after, the top half of a skull too heavy for any of the undernourished scavengers to move. It never enters his mind that it was once part of a human being. He drives the dogs away, picks it up, brings it over to the crippled animal, and stands guard while the gray bearded mongrel gnaws away at the delicacy, from time to time looking up to express gratitude to its benefactor. From then on wherever Roberto goes the dog follows; nothing can dissuade it. Finally the boy accepts that they will travel together, it's better than being alone.

It has to have a name, a name is an important thing. Roberto's mother and father would spend many evenings when the new ones were coming, saying aloud different names until one of them seemed right. Only with his infant brother did it happen differently. *Cesar*, his father announced right away. His wife nodded her head in agreement.

"Your name is Cesar," Roberto tells the dog.

That night he sleeps with his arm around his new companion. It is almost like having a blanket to keep him warm. In the morning they walk off together, the dog wagging his tail and struggling to keep pace with his new master. It is still ninety kilometers to Nuevo Loredo.

3

The maquiladora factories that sprung up after the NAFTA Treaty was signed, extend for over a mile on both sides of the highway leading into Nuevo Laredo: General Electric, Westinghouse, Sony, scores more Fortune five hundred corporations and the satellites that service them, here under the guise of free trade, for cheap labor.

Yolanda Garcia, just sixteen years old, works in the General Electric plant helping assemble eighty inch television sets that will sell in America for ten thousand dollars apiece. The production line reminds her of the mile long freight trains that rumbled by every night at three in the morning, so close to the room she shared with her three sisters that their flimsy bed shook. They lived in a shantytown on the outskirts of Mexico City, close to ancient ruins that spoke of the once proud heritage of her ancestors. A brick wall surrounded the compound so the depressing present wouldn't intrude on the romanticized past sold to tourists who came from all parts of the world to marvel at the remains of a civilization that had been destroyed by a foreign invader.

Her father and mother worked twelve hours a day, six days a week, doing menial work in the city. Yolanda took care of the younger children, worked a small plot of land in the community farm, did the laundry, mended clothes long past their life expectancy, and prepared the meager dinners. In a few months Sylvia, the next oldest, would be taking her place; Yolanda would work in the city, cleaning offices and toilets in a downtown building. Only if she got to America could she escape that lifetime sentence.

The look of pure innocence on Yolanda's face could only belong to the very young, but her full and sensuous figure made the journey possible; truck drivers were almost always grateful for company, particularly of the opposite sex. Most were fatherly and kind, a few times it was fortunate she was agile and deceptively strong. More than once neither was the case.

The separation from her family dispirited her, and sometimes she pressed her face into a pillow and wept silently. A veneer of self confidence soon replaced innocence, and concealed the insecurity and vulnerability that lay beneath the surface. To prove to the world that she was afraid of nothing or no one, she smoked, drank, and when the occasion suited her, bedded men.

An ominous threat now undermines her swagger: fear for her safety, for her life. It began with the unexplained disappearance of a female worker from the plant next to where she worked. A week later two bodies were discovered, one near the factory-owned dormitory where she slept, the other in the trash pile outside the General Electric Plant. The women had been raped, strangled, and disfigured.

4

The dog catches her attention. There used to be dozens of them on the streets, before the Veterinary College in Laredo started offering five dollars each for live specimens students could operate on. Five dollars was more that many citizens of Nuevo Laredo earned in a month.

At first glance the animal is humorous, a crooked leg points right at her, but Yolanda sees the way it looks warily in all directions, baring brown, worn down teeth and growling when anyone comes close to a boy standing beside it. The boy, hustling to wash the windshield of any car that stops at the one signal in town, is as ragged looking as a discarded piece of sugar cane.

When she wants to get someone's attention Yolanda whistles with two fingers in her mouth, the way not many men can do. The boy hurries over to her, it could be a job of some kind.

She points to a field, overgrown with weeds shoulder high, that slopes up beyond the town and disappears over a ridge.

"I don't like walking home alone. There's a burrito left over from yesterday."

Roberto nods his head: "My dog doesn't walk too fast."

"He's sure funny looking. Does he have a name?"

"Cesar."

She reaches down and runs her hand over his back.

"My name's Yolanda."

She lives in one of the dormitories the companies rent to their single employees; families live in homemade shacks scattered all across the area, squatters the corporate owners tolerate as long as they remain employees. The dormitories are pre-fab, windowless, storage-like structures partitioned into compartments that contain a cot, a table and a chair. Lavatories and a community kitchen are in a separate structure.

Yolanda watches as the boy eats the burrito slowly and methodically as if each piece is the last, with no certainty when there will be another; she herself often has to control the urge to bolt food down and quiet pangs of hunger. The dog of course has no such discipline and stares sadly at the vacant spot that had for a moment held his morsel of food.

"Where are you coming from?" It isn't hard to guess where they are headed.

"Guadeloupe. He started tagging along later."

With the urgency of someone who has had no one to talk to for weeks, words pour out of Roberto so rapidly that Yolanda has to ask him to slow down.

". . . and when no letter came for more than a month, my mother got afraid something bad happened. The priest told her not to worry, he was a good Christian, god would look after him. But when she read him the last letter, the priest got all red and said the union had turned father away from his family and from god."

"Wait until to-morrow to leave. It's Independence Day. There will be a celebration in Laredo, the police will be busy with the crowds."

"Why do they celebrate Mexican Independence in Texas?"

"Laredo was the capital when Texas and California were part of our country."

He nodded. He liked learning things like that.

"It's not easy to cross the border, you'll need a good night's rest. There's room on the bed."

She takes her nightdress out of a cardboard suitcase that serves as a closet, then a plain shift which she hands him:

"We're the same size."

She starts to step out of her dress, but the expression on Roberto's face stops her:

"You can close your eyes if you want."

He shakes his head, and Yolanda smiles.

"Would you like to kiss me?" she teases.

He shrugs.

She hesitates a moment: "Better you wait for someone else. Now turn around."

She slips into the night dress.

"Your turn. My eyes are shut tight."

The sight of Roberto in a dress makes them both burst out laughing. For a few minutes they are children again. The dog, eager to join in the festivities, beats a rhythm on the cement floor with his tail. Yolanda bends down and scratches behind his ears.

"I'll show you the toilet," she tells Roberto. "We'll bring back some newspaper for Cesar to sleep on."

The dog, with two masters now and nothing to threaten him, falls asleep at once. Roberto still has some things on his mind:

"Have you ever tried it? To sneak across the border?"

Yolanda has no wish to face the answer to that question again:

"It's too late for bedtime stories."

But the memory is not easily erased from her consciousness. While Roberto sleeps, she relives it for the hundredth time.

Two bridges cross the Rio Grande side by side: one for pedestrians, the other for vehicles. The river is several hundred yards wide but Yolanda can see U.S. inspectors on the other side, checking everyone's documents.

She stands for a long time below the bridge, clogged with trucks carrying goods from the maquiladora factories to America, some of them surely with television sets she has helped put together. She stares down at the river; the cesspool of rotting wood, refuse, and garbage would be really disgusting to go into, but only one thing stops her: she never had the chance to learn how to swim. There is no way for her to cross. Tears of anger and frustration fill her eyes.

"Hola."

Yolanda turns. For a fleeting moment she sees her father: "Papa. . . ."

The man smiles: "I am not so handsome."

"The white hair. . . ."

"We are both old men. Why are you so sad?"

She wipes away her tears: "I can't swim."

"The current is too strong for swimming. We'll walk."

He motions for her to follow him, and heads downstream.

"Half a mile past the bridges the river turns south on its way to the Gulf of Mexico. There is a sandbar. Crossing it isn't easy, the current breeches the bar in different places, you can't tell in advance where. More than one compadre has slipped and disappeared."

You can tell where the sandbar is, the water is all smooth, like a lake.

"Watch and do as I do," he tells her.

After each small step he stops, one foot at a time gingerly tests the terrain ahead. It takes twenty minutes to cross the river, an agonizing eternity for a non-swimmer surrounded by water ten feet deep. When they reach the shore Yolanda is trembling, and sobs escape her lips.

"Control yourself," the man orders, "there is still danger."

It is a steep climb up the bank of the river. When they reach the top they are in the middle of a flat field that has recently been plowed; rolls of cut hay, taller than a man, are dispersed across it in perfect geometric order. The city is visible in the distance.

The man is breathing hard, and Yolanda sees that he is even older than her father. He walks quickly and silently to the nearest bale of hay, and sits down behind it.

"We can rest here a minute."

"You've done this before," Yolanda says matter of factly.

He nods.

"Why did you come back?"

"My wife was sick."

Yolanda thinks it better not to ask any more questions. They sit in silence. When his breathing returns to normal he rises to his feet.

"One mountain lion can elude the hunter, two together make an inviting target." He points ahead: "The highway is on the other side of the city. When I leave count to thirty. If it is still quiet follow me, if not don't move from here until after dark. Buena suerte."

She hears the gunshot before she gets to fifteen. Then sounds she remembers from a time the family worked on a ranch and a runaway steer was wrestled to the ground.

Men are coming towards her, getting closer. She can hear them talk. "There's another one! I saw two!"

Yolanda is restless in bed all night. Roberto, for the first time since he left home, sleeps without the knife in his hands, the dreamless sleep perhaps enjoyed by soon to be born fetuses safe in their mothers' sanctuary. It isn't known if animals dream, or if they do whether their dreams disappear without a trace, like clouds that pass overhead, or the songs of birds in flight, but Cesar too sleeps well.

5

When Roberto awakens, Yolanda is dressed. She tells him all that she learned from the man who reminded her of her father, then hands him a coin:

"Menudo gives the most nourishment for a peso. There's a stand by the traffic light. I can't be late for work, but you wait here until the celebration begins. Buena suerte."

She bends down and strokes the dog:

"You won't make it if you take him with you."

Roberto knows it's true.

"Will you keep him?" He asks urgently.

Yolanda feels a kind of affection for the animal, and pity. She knows what is in store for him whichever answer she gives.

"You wouldn't have to be afraid anymore," Roberto pleads.

"Where would he go when I work? People pick up stray dogs and sell them."

"Cesar will know his enemies."

Yolanda looks down at the dog that is leaning now against Roberto's leg. She herself needs to be free of responsibility; one day she will try again to get to America. She shakes her head and goes out the door.

At the crest of the hill she looks back; the boy and his dog are outside, watching her. Yolanda sees in them her own loneliness, and pain shoots through her as if she stuck her hand in a hot fire. Maybe one of us will be lucky, she thinks, puts two fingers to her lips, and whistles.

Cesar raises himself to a standing position. He recognizes a command when he receives one, and looks up at the boy. Roberto signals for him to follow the girl. Life has long ago taught the dog to accept whatever opportunities are offered him; he hesitates a moment then lumbers after the girl, his head hung low. Three times he stops and looks back at the boy who has been so kind to him, then he raises his head and limps as fast as he can to catch up to his new master.

Cesar is the first to hear the fireworks. At the crest of the hill he begins to bark furiously.

Roberto goes back inside and changes into his own clothes. He spreads the shift Yolanda gave him to sleep in, neatly across the bed, and smoothes it out the way he has often seen his mother do. Then he tucks the knife into the waistband of his trousers.

Which Will Grow?

The motorcade, thirty old model cars, mostly Chevrolets, turned off the freeway onto a two lane highway that wound its way up the Tehachapi mountains. I hadn't been on this road before, and surveyed everything in sight as if I were moving into a new and strange neighborhood.

The ranches on both sides of the highway seemed straight out of a cowboy movie: barbed wire fences confined cattle grazing in slow motion; elaborate archways straddled driveways that led to homes barely visible in the distance.

The road narrowed and we drove onto a wooden bridge that crossed a small lake. The wooden planks rattled, and I was seized with a sudden anxiety, a foreboding that something hostile was lurking around the bend.

A short distance beyond the lake we entered a tunnel that had been carved through the mountain; I couldn't see where it ended. I wasn't afraid of the dark but my body grew rigid, as if to ward off a blow.

"Where are you taking me?"

"You'll see soon enough."

When we exited the tunnel the light blinded me at first, but as we rounded a bend, I could see the valley floor; the distant farmland was like the patchwork pattern of a homemade quilt. I tried to make out anything familiar, but the layer of haze that hovered over the ground made it difficult.

Then, as though I was peering through a high-powered tele-scope, I saw the shack my family used to rent from the owner of the strawberry fields. The girl inside was nine years old, thin as a rail.

"*Come home straight from school.*"

"*Yes, momma.*"

The motorcade pulled up in front of a large wrought-iron gate, the only way in to the property enclosed by a chain link fence. Above the gate was a sign, weather-beaten and rusted but still legible:

State Sanitarium

When the sanitarium, rendered obsolete by antibiotics, was put up for auction, we made certain no one went anywhere near the place until a couple from Los Angeles, longtime sup-porters of the union, was able to buy it for us; the right wing ranchers in the area would have paid any price had they known Mexican and Filipino field hands might become their neigh-bors.

A banner was draped hastily over the old sign. Letters six feet high read:

LA PAZ

We would soon see the Union's new headquarters, a place where itinerant farmworkers from across the state would be able to meet and exchange ideas about how the union could best serve their needs.

My husband stood at the gate waiting for me to join him. No matter how eager to see this dream of a lifetime come true, Cesar Chavez, my life's partner, would not step foot onto his new home without me.

"Is anything wrong, Helen?"

My mother kissed me and joined my father in the raitero's truck that drove them to the fields to pick strawberries until it got too dark to tell which ones were ripe. The sun hadn't yet come up.

Halfway to school, a car pulled up beside me and honked its horn. The window was rolled down.

"I want to talk to you."

The man's voice didn't sound friendly. I shook my head and kept walking.

The car pulled ahead and stopped. The man got out and waited for me. He was big and fat, and his face was full of pockmarks.

"Hungry?"

"No."

"You look like you're hungry."

I tried to walk on but he blocked my way.

"Let me go by. I'll be late for school."

"I'll write you a note," he said and laughed.

I turned and started to run away, but he grabbed me and lifted me off my feet.

I fought and kicked as hard as I could but he held me under one arm, opened the car door, threw me hard onto the front seat, and slammed the door shut. I tried to open it and get out. When I came to my head hurt, and we were part way up a mountain.

"Try anything again I'll whack you a good one."

"Where are you taking me?"

"You'll see soon enough."

We came to a small lake, and drove over a narrow bridge. The planks creaked. A mother duck watched her little ones duck their heads under water looking for food. It was funny the way they flipped over, their tails pointing straight up in the air, but I wasn't in the mood to smile.

The car entered a tunnel. I couldn't see where it ended. When we came out I could see the whole valley below. My mother and father were down there picking strawberries. I called out to them for help, but they were too far away to hear me.

We turned onto a narrow dirt road. Most of the farms we worked on had entrances like that. The road dead ended at a chain link fence that went in both directions, the only way past it was through a wrought iron gate. Over the gate was a sign. A dozen large black birds were perched on it and I could only make out the first letter, an 'S.'

The moment the gate began to open, the birds, angry at having been disturbed, spread their wings and dived towards the car, rising in formation barely a foot away as we drove through.

A man in a white coat led me into an office. It smelled like the chemicals I was once given to scrub the floor of a milking barn.

"Where am I?"

"The State TB sanitarium."

"What's TB?"

"Tuberculosis. A disease."

"Why am I here?"

"You look like you could be sick."

"I'm not. I want to go home."

"People with TB have to be quarantined."

"What's quarantined?"

"Means no one gets in to see you, you don't get out. It's easy to catch."

"I'm not sick. I told you."

"You're better off here. Three meals a day. And the work's a lot easier than you're used to."

The room they put me in had two rows of cots, thirty in all. Half of them were empty. I recognized a girl a few years older than me, her family picked grapes near us a couple of years ago. She told me the hospital got paid by the number of patients, so they went into poor neighborhoods and picked up skinny kids."

"How long are they kept here?" I asked her.

She shrugged:

"Two years so far. I'm lucky. Lots get sick while they're here. And die."

The lights were turned out, the door locked. They wouldn't get to see me cry. Not one tear. I shut my eyes tight so I wouldn't forget things that happened before.

I thought about yesterday. Sunday. When there was no school the whole family did farm work. My brother and sister were sorting strawberries with my mother, I was sowing seeds in a field with my father.

I asked him if he could tell which seeds would grow and which would not.

"Only god knows."

If I wasn't going to die in here, it would be up to me, not god.

I forced myself to sleep, but when it came it wasn't peaceful.

A flock of large birds was flying in winged formation across a cloudless sky. Suddenly one of them soared free. The others flapped their wings furiously, doing their best to catch up. But one could not and fell behind, separated from the flock. A shot rang out. The bird's wing was broken. The bird that had forged ahead turned back. He circled the wounded bird, trying to hold it up in the air, but it plummeted to the ground.

Some nights the dream took different forms: the large birds could be tiny, they could be butterflies; the bullet might be a rock or an arrow. But the end was always the same.

Cesar called to me:

"Helen, aren't you well?"

Dear Cesar. How many crates of lettuce had we picked side by side with our children? How many nervous trigger fingers away from death have we survived together? But the nightmares were mine alone. I couldn't walk through those gates. Not ever again.

The workers were out of their cars, waiting to follow Cesar and me through the gate to their promised land.

An old man, a Filipino lured with hundreds of others to America by ranchers looking for cheap labor, began to chant the union's mantra:

para vivir!

Casa buena!

Con el union venceramos.

Others joined in, some in Spanish, some in English:

A living wage!

Decent housing!

With the union we will succeed!

Health benefits!

An end to child labor!

With the union we will succeed!

At that moment I understood that it wasn't about Cesar or me, it wasn't about his dream or my nightmare. It was about the men, women and children who spend their lives bent over the ground, picking the earth's bounty for unseen owners. It was about the workers who sacrifice their health, their youth, their innocence, for the chance merely to survive.

The past belonged to memory. The future belonged to hope. To La Paz.

I got out of the car, and walked over to my husband. We clenched hands, raised them skyward, and walked through the gate.

Masquerade

AUTHOR'S NOTE: My wife was the one who suggested to Cesar that the Union acquire a property and replicate the model and ideals of a kibbutz. After we transferred title to them, he told her what had happened to his wife when she was a child.

Have A Nice Day

1

Margo's father was a quiet man, almost unnoticed wherever he went. Even at family gatherings Max Gross rarely spoke, and when he did the gentle tone seemed a contradiction. Of average height but muscular, from the day he immigrated from Russia he chose physical labor to more genteel occupations that would have exposed an inner shame that he couldn't master the new language. All his thoughts and energies were devoted to providing a decent life for his family. Though many judged him an unsuccessful man, he was fully satisfied with his life.

It was his beloved wife's birthday, and Max had invited a small group of their friends to dinner at a popular Jewish restaurant on the Lower East Side. He could barely wait to give her the present he had carefully hidden for over a month. By some standards the one and a half karat diamond ring might not be impressive, but to Max it meant he had reached a respectable level of success in his adopted country, and he was proud. 'A diamond is forever,' had special meaning to those for whom life in America was difficult.

Max was meticulous in everything he did. For this special night he went through every shirt and tie to be sure which went best with the new suit he bought for the occasion, and he laid the complete outfit carefully over the bed. It didn't happen often that he sang in the shower. Mrs. Gross recognized the Yiddish song, and hummed along; it was going to be a *freilich* evening.

Suddenly the singing stopped. For a brief moment there was silence, then the dull thud of a heavy object hitting the floor. Mrs. Gross found the diamond ring in the pocket of the jacket Max would wear when the casket lowered his body into the ground.

For weeks after the funeral, Margo's mother rarely left her apartment, the only remaining connection to the man with whom she had shared the better part of her life. A prisoner in the solitary confinement of despair, she existed in an aimless vacuum, refusing to read a newspaper, listen to the radio, or watch television. That changed when she learned from her daughter that Israel was at war with its neighbors. She and Max had planned to make a trip there in the fall; now she felt more than curiosity. The Jewish Agency for Palestine, an organization that helped make arrangements for people wanting to emigrate to Israel, had its office only a few blocks from the apartment. She was there first thing in the morning.

"I think you should at least wait until things settle down a little," Margo urged when she learned her mother's plan. "The war's barely over. No one can say for sure what's going to happen now."

"Another war has to be waged. . . . for peace. It too needs fighters."

"Mother, you're. . . ."

"Too old? I'm a socialist! What you believe in matters, not age."

Margo knew that when her mother's mind was made up there was no changing it. As soon as the paperwork was completed Mrs. Gross left for Israel.

Every night before she put Randy to sleep, Margo read to him. He loved fables and fairy tales, but he was almost six and she felt he was ready to hear about real people who were different from those he was used to seeing. For her thirteenth birthday her father had given her a subscription to National Geographic, and renewed it every year until he died. Margo saved all of them and picked an article she thought would be appropriate for her son.

It was about a Stone Age Tribe that had recently been discovered on a remote island in the Philippines. A surveyor for a logging company searching for the giant mahogany trees thought to exist deep in the jungle, had stumbled upon natives who'd never before seen anyone other than the forty or so men, women, and children who lived together peacefully in one family group. Before long there would be many strangers in their midst.

Randy was fascinated by the story and by one image in particular: the photograph of a dark skinned boy wearing only a loin cloth and sailing what seemed to be a kite. It was a leash made of leaves, attached to it a butterfly.

"It looks fun but there aren't any butterflies in New York," he said sadly.

"This summer we'll visit grandma. I'll bet there are lots of butterflies in Israel."

"I'll put three on one leash, the way the man does who walks dogs on the street." He stared at the picture: "What will happen to the boy now?"

"His life will change."

"I want everything to stay the way it is."

2

Just as they were getting ready to leave for the airport to pick up her mother, Margo got a call from the Department of Parks and Recreation.

"They screwed up and gave our time to another birthday party," she told Randy. As soon as we get back I'll have to go down there and work something out."

Driving back from the airport she told her mother what had happened.

"Are you okay alone with Randy? I mean maybe you'd like to rest. I can take him with me."

Mrs. Gross suspected that somewhere in that question was a payback for the time she told her expectant daughter not to count on her for baby sitting.

"On the kibbutz I sometimes take care of forty little ones." And with a twinkle in her eye added: "Old people do change."

After Margo left, Mrs. Gross asked Randy to help her unpack; a pull-down couch did little to convert Margo's office into a bedroom, he could suggest where her things could be put. He was proudly playing the host when he saw something wrapped in fancy paper half buried in the suitcase.

"Is it for me?"

"Yes."

"I want to open it."

"You have to wait for the party."

"That's not until day after to-morrow." He thought a moment: "If I do something that really fools you, can I have a wish?"

Mrs. Gross smiled and nodded.

He went to his mother's desk and took out a large piece of paper and two pencils. With one in each hand he drew simultaneously the numbers three, four and five, then handed the paper to her:

"Read these," he challenged.

Mrs. Gross studied the paper.

"I can only read the column on the right."

Randy pointed to a mirror that hung on the wall near the entry:

"Hold it up."

His grandmother did as he asked.

"Now the right side is backward. That's amazing."

"Nobody else in kindergarten can do it," he said proudly. "I get my wish."

Inside the box were two miniature figures made of plastic. One was of a small boy, the other of a giant. In the boy's hand was a sling-shot mounted on a spring. Mrs. Gross demonstrated how it worked:

"When you release the spring the giant falls to the ground. We make these at the Kibbutz."

She told him the story of David and Goliath:

"It's a reminder to all of us, that good can win out . . . no matter the odds."

Randy's hearing was fine tuned to the sound of the key, and he was at the door the moment his mother opened it.

"Mommy! I got a present from grandma!"

"Has he been a handful?" Margo asked her mother as he ran into his bedroom.

"We're getting along fine. As long as I let him have his way."

Randy came back holding the present behind his back:
"Close your eyes."

"I have to make some calls first. The mothers have to be told the new time for the party."

Randy wasn't thrilled with the delay and began to sulk, his lower lip trembling just enough to make clear he was fighting back tears. The tactic usually got him what he wanted but Margo didn't want to reinforce her mother's not so subtle suggestion that her son was spoiled.

"It will have to wait."

The harsh tone confused Randy. He handed the gift to his grandmother and marched out of the room.

The party was a paean of disorder. No activity held the attention of the boys for more than a few minutes, until the fathers began showing up to take their families home. There was still some time left so a new game was organized: they seated their kids on their shoulders, then sort of like jousting, used them in a game of tag. Randy watched, annoyed that he was left out of the fun. He knew he was different from the other kids, his father was the man in the picture frame on his mother's desk, but he never really missed having a father before.

One of the fathers, noticing that the birthday boy was unhappy, put his son down and came over to Randy:

"Your turn." He cupped his hands. "Step into the stirrup and climb aboard."

Randy shook his head:

"Don't want to."

He marched over to where the gifts were arranged in a pile, and announced that he was going to start opening them.

The game of tag was called off and everyone gathered around him. He picked up his grandmother's present, now carefully re-wrapped, and took it out of the box with a flourish.

"It's from Israel," he declared proudly.

His friends found the toy only mildly interesting and called out for him to open the presents they had brought.

He was quiet all the way home. When they got to the apartment, Margo took a photograph album from her desk drawer, and removed a snapshot of a man holding a small child on his shoulders. She brought it over to her still brooding son.

"Your father loved you very much. Every night at bed time, he put you on his shoulders, turned on a Mozart piece, and danced around the room with you until you fell asleep."

He bit his lip, determined not to cry:

"I don't remember."

"You were too little, then."

"I like it better when you read me a story."

Alone with her mother for the first time that day, Margo put the photograph back into the album.

"I took that the night before Jim left for Washington. I think those were the happiest moments of his life."

"Happy isn't something familiar to you anymore, is it?"

"I'm happy that you're here."

"That's not what I mean. There comes a time when mourning dishonors the one you've lost. I'm tempted to say I know how it feels but that would be unfair. As you grow older you're better prepared."

She leafed through the album until one photograph caught her attention:

"It's outside the Supreme Court Building isn't it."

Margo nodded: "He was about to try his first case there, the dream of a lifetime come true. You would have approved. He was defending a prisoner's right to have his ideas published. In this case unpopular ones. The prisoner was George Jackson." Her mother nodded. "When he left for Washington he was too excited to tie his necktie and I had to do it for him. I wanted to come with him, to watch him, but he said it would make him more nervous. I could have insisted . . . I should have. . . ."

"Who doesn't wish they could have, should have . . . always when it's too late. I didn't appreciate that your father was idealistic in his own way. He believed in things like honesty, loyalty. And love." Tears began to well in her eyes. "Old people are too easily overcome by sentimentality. It's not becoming."

Margo changed the subject:

"I haven't asked if you enjoyed the party."

"I was hoping you would. I may have opened my mouth anyway."

"Flattery was never your strong suit so it's probably not something I want to hear."

"It's not easy to have things pointed out that you'd rather not see."

"I'm ready."

"What floor is the apartment on? Seventy? I have a mental block every time I get on the elevator. You know I was never crazy about heights . . . just thinking about your father working all day on a rooftop used to make me dizzy."

"Fifty-one," Margo replied.

"When you look down, the people are so small they're like little toys. Not real."

"This isn't about how high up we live."

"It is . . . in a way. You live in a world populated by a privileged few. The only kids my impressionable grandson ever sees are spoiled."

"Just because they weren't interested in David and Goliath?" Margo challenged.

"That's beneath you. All they see are rich kids. It won't take long for them to become little snobs, little snobs grow into elitists."

"The only decent schools in the city are unaffordable for your working class. I didn't make it that way. And I don't know of any kibbutzes in Manhattan," Margo replied defensively.

Mrs. Gross shrugged: "I've said my piece."

Margo resented that her right to be satisfied with the life she and Jim had created for themselves was being challenged. It wasn't the first time she bristled at her mother's unwillingness to overlook things she deemed wrong, no matter how sensitive the issue might be. When Mrs. Gross left for Israel the sadness of separation was tinged with relief.

3

On the first day of spring Margo received an elegantly embossed envelope in the mail:

You are cordially invited to attend a celebration on the occasion of Jennifer Adams being named Television Personality of the Year.

Saturday April Twentieth.

Eight P.M. until. . . .
Tavern on the Park.
Formal Attire.
RSVP by April Tenth.'
Handwritten across the bottom of the invitation was:
'Please come . . .
Jennifer.'
Why not? Margo thought. She was curious about the sudden gesture of friendship from her old boss.

'Tavern in the Park,' the newest 'in' spot in the city, was hardly a tavern. Large enough to accommodate several hundred guests, the decor was an interior decorator's fantasy: too much gilt and glitter, zero subtlety, plush but uncomfortable. The setting however was breath taking: thousands of tiny lights that outlined the building as well as the trees that surrounded it created the aura of a Fairyland.

The room was overflowing with well wishers and envious competitors vying with one another to be seen and heard. Silver tubs filled with caviar were scattered around the room, waiters dressed in black wove their way through the crowds offering exotic hors d'oeuvres. Margo took in the scene, fascinated by the skill with which the guests feigned having a wonderful time; the laughter and chatter were as false as the cleavage many of the women had on display.

"Margo."

The honoree, surveying her incoming guests as carefully as an experienced shopper sorting through a rack of clothes on sale, was coming towards her.

"How good of you to come."

"Thanks for the invite."

"You don't thank an old friend. I brag to everyone whenever I see your byline. I call you my protégé. You don't mind, do you?"

Margo shook her head, and smiled:

"You haven't changed."

"Do I take that as a compliment?"

The answer was preempted by a man who hurried over to them, leaned close to Jennifer and whispered into her ear: "*Newsweek.*"

"My show's account exec," Jennifer told Margo. "I have to run dear. Tony will give you an intro if there's anybody you want to meet."

He smiled as she hurried off, obviously accustomed to frenetic behavior. Margo noted that he wore his position well—lean and fit, suit tailored just enough, not too high style to stand out above the guests.

"Hi. I'm Tony De Marco. Jennifer speaks well of you."

"We haven't seen or spoken to one another in years," Margo said dryly.

Characteristic of successful executives is the ability to hear only what they want, undeterred from the pursuit of their immediate objective.

"We're hoping you'll profile her."

"Selling celebrities is not my forte."

"It's my job to convince you otherwise." He smiled at her. "It's a very pleasant assignment. As is talking about Jennifer. Hers is an extraordinary story . . . you could say a female 'Rocky' who rose like a meteor from a local station to network anchor.

"It didn't happen quite like that. Rocky had to fight his way up and took some pretty hard licks."

He smiled in the way a fighter who's just taken a good lick himself tries to show he hasn't been hurt:

"We need to get to know one another better. How about dinner to-morrow."

Margo had gone out on a few blind dates since Jim died. None of them turned out well but she knew she wasn't blameless. Right now a diversion was welcome, she'd give it one more try.

Over dinner he told her that he also handled Pepsi Cola, and how he'd just gotten them to convert an empty warehouse in Long Island into a state of the art film studio.

"Filmed TV is the way to go. With the time differential across the country, the only way to get prime viewing every-where is if you're on film and syndicated. To-morrow I'm lunching with Faye Emerson, she'd be the perfect host for a daytime strip. I'll have to let her know that our target audi-ence is female mental defectives with curlers in their hair, and that she'd have to pretend she was one of them." He held up his hand defensively: "Only kidding."

In a kind of stupor of disinterest and boredom, Margo found it simpler just to let the fatuous remark pass.

After dinner he took her to the exclusive disco, 'Studio 54.' Outside the club, confined in a roped off area by a three hun-dred pound guard, paparazzi, autograph hounds, and group-ies cheered as celebrities arrived in limousines. Among them that night were Bianca Jagger, Andy Warhol, and Liza Minelli.

Inside, music thundering out of a dozen huge speakers assaulted the senses, and the uninhibited among the guests danced and postured with abandon. Fashion models showing their bodies to best advantage, treated the mirrored environs of the club like runways.

Margo opted to be a spectator. When Tony returned from the bar with two glasses of champagne she asked him about one barely clothed woman who was the center of much attention.

"This month's Playboy Centerfold."

It struck Margo that Jim would never have come to a place like this. He hated chic and celebrity and what it did to people. What kept her from walking out?

"Something wrong?" Tony asked.

"I was just reminded of something."

"Some thing . . . or some one?"

"Both actually."

"If you want to forget your troubles the bathroom attendants deal coke."

She shook her head:

"I really don't want to forget."

When Margo thought back over the evening she wasn't sure if she'd had three or four glasses of champagne. Twice Tony excused himself and headed for the men's room. When he returned the last time he seemed different and she wondered if he'd snorted coke.

"We have two choices," he announced, "move onward and upward, or bring down the curtain. Your call."

Margo had reached this crossroad before and been hesitant to dishonor Jim. This time the red light was obscured by alcohol and the erotic tableau.

The suite the agency kept at the Waldorf might have been used for client conferences but Margo wasn't too high to guess it's real purpose. Tony leafed through a collection of CD's.

"How about Sondheim? Have you seen 'Company'?"
Margo shook her head.

Too close to home he thought on reflection, and put some mood music on. He went over to the fully equipped bar, poured two drinks and handed her one:

"Thirty year old Scotch."

"I think I've had enough to drink."

"You're like a virgin bride on her wedding night. It's quite charming."

He cupped his hand under her chin and kissed her. She didn't respond, and he studied her a moment:

"Look if you're not up to this . . . it's no big deal."

Margo wanted to shout back that it sure as hell was a big deal for her. She thought about walking out again but felt challenged. Her whole life had become a challenge, her work, her mother, her son, the shackles of widowhood.

She remembered little about the actual lovemaking if you could call it that. In spite of Tony's determination there was no passion and little enjoyment. Added to that he wouldn't wear a condom.

"All the pleasure goes to a piece of latex."

She hated herself for letting him have his way, and loathed what she had done that evening. Being normal didn't mean making her body available to any jerk. That night sleep eluded her. She had the grotesque sensation that he was still inside her, and made her way to the toilet; maybe she could flush it out. The ugliness wouldn't go away and she downed a sleeping pill.

It was cancer. She knew it. She hated the gynecologist who spread her open like a turkey getting ready for stuffing. But it had to be cut out. The subway would get her to the hospital on time. A crush of people tried to beat her into the car, already so packed it didn't seem possible any more could get inside. The train lurched forward. She was wedged in so tightly she couldn't move a muscle. A man's hand began to fondle her breasts from behind. No one paid any attention when she cried for help.

The hangover in the morning was more from an excess of depression than from alcohol. On the way to work a woman sat on the landing half way down into the subway terminal where Margo caught the 'E' train going cross-town. One hand held an infant, the other begged for a coin. The rush of people hurrying down the steps made it difficult to stop and open her purse but Margo did, and added: "I hope you have a good day."

She'd have felt better if she could have taken back those trite words.

. . .and hope to die

Brigadier General Randolph Cummins, a second generation West Point graduate much decorated for bravery in World War II, took for granted that his son would continue the family tradition. The young man had no enthusiasm for a career in the army, but from the time his mother left her husband and three year old son, never to be heard from again, Randolph Cummins Jr. walked the path paved with his father's wishes.

At the Point he distinguished himself by graduating third from the top of his class. When you consider that Dwight D. Eisenhower, one of his father's classmates, ranked third from the bottom and went on to become President of the United States, you would have high expectations for Cummins' advancement, but he chose to pursue justice rather than combat, and embarked on an undistinguished career defending soldiers accused of crimes as petty as curfew violation, as odorous as desertion; not the sort of accomplishments that encouraged promotion.

His first assignment outside of the Pentagon was to a Special Services Unit in Vietnam charged with providing newsworthy items that could be used to reassure the public the war was going well. Second Lieutenant Cummins didn't adapt well to his new environment, and began having migraine headaches. One particularly severe attack occurred during a meeting in Saigon with the publisher of the city's leading newspaper. The Lieutenant was taken to a nearby hospital, and fell in love with Sung Hee, the nurse who attended him. When it became clear that Saigon was about to fall, he persuaded her to leave with him on a helicopter evacuating VIPs from the country.

The General, who saw no difference between 'Orientals' of any nationality and the Japanese he fought in his war, did not attend his son's wedding, nor would he set foot in his house. Once a week they had lunch at the Officer's Club, but Sung Hee was never mentioned.

Randolph and Sung Hee had one trait in common: troubled feelings were closely held, covered by a callous of outward calm. For Sung Hee it was a tradition of her culture and class; for Randolph a discipline taught by his father and nourished by military training. Undercurrents swirled beneath the placid waters of their marriage. Sung Hee resented Randolph for separating her from her family, and for accepting his father's affront. Randolph saw Sung Hee as a moat that separated him from his father. Still the marriage remained afloat, and in a few years they had a daughter they named Angelica, for she did have the face of an angel.

The North Tower of Walter Reed Hospital admits only the highest echelon of government officials and Army personnel; it would not be far afield to liken it to the Waldorf Astoria's Tower, doctors and nurses, most in the military, substituting for maitres'd and butlers. Randolph brought his daughter when he came there to visit his father, recovering from prostate surgery. She was three years old; the General would be seeing her for the first time.

When the precocious child entered the room, she mimicked what she saw her father do, came to attention and saluted. Before the visit ended, the General was completely disarmed by his granddaughter, and promised to do as she asked, come to her house to see their Christmas tree as soon as he came out of the hospital. She hoped it would be soon because 'the smell of medicine isn't nice'.

The General brooded over his new status as a grandfather: he would have to accept his daughter-in-law as part of the family; he needed to find something special to give his granddaughter for Christmas. The second day home, the Post ran a picture on the front page of the five-story Christmas tree in Rockefeller Plaza. That was it.

He called Angelica's mother, and as if it were a routine conversation, said he'd like to take the child to New York to see the famous tree in person.

"We'll window shop on Fifth Avenue, she can pick out her own Christmas present. I'll want to show her off at the Officers' Club, but with the staff jet I can have her back in time for dinner."

Sung Hee accepted the truce on his terms. She understood well the value of a grandparent to a child. To Randolph the turn of events came as a great relief.

The Federal Aviation investigation concluded that the Lear Jet, touching down on the runway, struck a piece of debris from the commercial aircraft that landed a few minutes earlier. The General's plane veered off the landing strip, turned over and burst into flames. Angelica was the only survivor but she never regained consciousness and died three days later.

***

Only a few years short of retirement, Randolph finally reached the rank of Lt. Colonel. When Congress passed the Freedom of Information Act, he was put in charge of the department set up to handle requests for the release of classified documents. His directive, though unwritten, was to grant only what was absolutely necessary in order to be in compliance with the law; what individual citizens wanted to know paled beside the protection secrecy provided the government. 'National security' was the barrier supplicants would have to breach.

Randolph was assigned an Aide, a Master Sergeant. It didn't take long for him to figure out that the Sergeant's real job was to keep the Pentagon informed about what was going on in the office; he would have to watch his rear for what was euphemistically referred to in the military as 'friendly fire.'

Cummins was stunned to discover that in the previous year alone, fourteen million documents were designated by the government as secret! It was no surprise then that hundreds of letters poured in every week requesting release of classified files. Many were frivolous, some by their naiveté without merit, a few were modest and approved. The response to the others was 'under consideration'; the time it would take, indeterminate.

Conscientious to a fault, the Colonel read every application. It was an unchallenging job, free of stress, and he grew more cheerful than he'd been for a long while. Memorial Day weekend was coming up, he and Sung Hee could take a short trip. They hadn't been to Atlantic City in years. She liked roulette, maybe he'd try it too. There were only a few submissions remaining, he'd leave early for a change.

Most of the letters were typewritten on stationary with letterheads from law offices, publications, or businesses; this was on plain, lined paper, written in a hurried hand that suggested urgency. It was from a discharged Army Reservist recently back from Iraq. The soldier had served in a Military Police Brigade.

He read it a second time, then went to the secure computer that gave him access to all but the most sensitive documents. The search took longer than usual. What finally came up startled him and he stared at the screen in disbelief. He waited until the Aide left for the day, put the Reservist's letter in his briefcase, and hurried out of the building.

After dinner he went to his study and sat deep in thought. He was at a crossroads; there were no signs, no map to point the way. When the housekeeper who left every night after doing the dishes had gone, he asked Sung Hee to join him.

She listened attentively as he read her the soldier's letter.

'. . . .the camera was confiscated by the same Intelligence Officer who told me to take the pictures. What was done to prisoners at Abu Ghraib may one day come to light, and I could be accused of being responsible. The photographs will show that I was obeying orders, and will be critical to my defense.'

"Did you know this was going on?" Sung Hee asked.

"No. Not until I saw the photographs. How can I describe them to you? There are about sixty in all. American soldiers, men and women both, tormenting terrified prisoners . . . some of it is obscene. Others, officers included, watch gleefully like it's a big party."

Sung Hee shook her head: "How can people see evil in front of their eyes but do nothing about it?"

"Last week on Meet the Press, a panelist questioned the Secretary of Defense's claim that Iraqis would eventually accept having American troops stationed in their country. The Secretary replied, 'People can be gotten used to anything.'"

"Have you?" Sung Hee asked.

"I got used to my life. I haven't forgotten the pain."

Randolph walked slowly to a wall safe, stood before it a few seconds, then opened it and took out an envelope yellow with age.

"I wrote this letter thirty five years ago. To the Inspector General."

He handed it to her.

"I never sent it."

When she began to read he walked out of the study.

The events I will describe were witnessed by me on June Eleven, 1969. On that day I decided to accompany the unit photographer assigned to do a photo shoot of a company commanded by Lieutenant John Calley.

"Do we do the interview now or later?" he asked when we arrived. I told him we didn't interview, pictures told the story we wanted to tell. "And tell no lies, cross your heart and hope to die," he said and laughed. Most officers know we inflate the number of enemy killed, by taking several pictures of each body. The photographers move them from place to place, change their position, add props. I heard one say to a dead body, "Smile you're on Candid Camera."

"Take lots of film. We're going to take out a Cong village called Mai Lai," the Lieutenant said. *(In Vietnamese Mai Lai means good fortune).*

After the artillery barrage things were quiet and I said to Calley "there's no enemy fire, now what?" He turned to his men and shouted: "Let's go!" They moved through the hamlet. There were long bursts of automatic fire, hand grenades were thrown, M-79 launchers hurled bomblets through the air. The troops were firing on anything that moved, at pigs, chickens, ducks, cows. Soldiers yelled inside huts for people to come out. If there was no answer they threw in grenades. The photographer and I followed one soldier into a hut which had been raked with bullets. There were three children inside . . . a woman with a wound in her side, and an old man squatting down, seriously wounded in both legs. From six feet the soldier aimed his forty five pistol and pulled the trigger, blowing the top of the old man's head off. I asked him why he did it. He said "this is war."

An old man wearing a straw coolie hat and no shirt was with a water buffalo in a paddy fifty yards away. He put his hands in the air. For no reason a soldier stabbed him through the heart with his bayonet, then grabbed another man, shot him in the neck and threw him into a well, lobbing a grenade in after him. "Way to do it," the Captain called out.

The killing once it began, created a chain reaction. Our soldiers were out of control. Families that huddled together for safety were mown down with automatic fire or blown apart by grenades. I couldn't watch anymore and wandered away. The next thing I saw was a sergeant forcing a young woman to perform oral sex on him. It was just behind a banana tree. He held a gun at her daughter's head, threatening to kill her. Lieutenant Calley happened along and told him to pull up his pants and get over to where the action was. He told me to follow him.

We came to a clearing where prisoners were being held, fifty or sixty squatting villagers guarded by some soldiers, men with beards, a handful of gray-haired women, children . . . babies to early teens. "I thought I told you to take care of them," Calley said. "Fire when I do."

They stood only ten feet away, changing magazines when needed. The Vietnamese screamed and tried to get up. Mothers threw themselves on top of the young ones in a desperate bid to protect them. One soldier started weeping. Tears flooded down his cheeks. When it was all over Calley turned to me calmly and said "OK. Let's go."

I will testify under oath that the events recounted here are true.

Sung Hee found her husband in the garden. He seemed to have aged ten years. She came over and touched his hand.

"I tried thinking I was different from Calley, from the others," he said softly. "Not doing anything wrong, just watching. But I knew that wasn't true. I was part of it. I've had to live with that."

"Will you grant that soldier's request for his photographs?"

"The Pentagon forbids anything that shows the war in an unpleasant light. Even pictures of coffins returning casualties for burial are banned."

He pointed to a lady bug on a nearby camellia bush.

"I'm like that bug. Incapable of distinguishing what's true and what's false, what's right, what's wrong. My efforts have been devoted to deceiving myself and others, and to avoid noticing it. I've been afraid all my life. I was afraid of failing my father. I was afraid of failing the soldiers. I was afraid of losing you. I was afraid to send the letter you just read. I went on that photo shoot because I was afraid I was a coward. I could no longer watch the war from an office in Saigon. I needed to breath the air of valor and bravery. I didn't find it."

He closed his eyes as though to shut out the past. His shoulders sagged, his body swayed slightly. Sung Hee wished she could pull him out of the quicksand of remorse, but she could not. If there was an analgesic for his pain he'd have to find it himself.

For a few minutes they didn't speak. Randolph gazed out at the garden.

"Your roses are beautiful."

He looked at her intently, as though he were seeing her for the first time.

"You're beautiful, Sung Hee."

Colonel Cummins was suddenly very tired. He touched her shoulder as he passed her on his way back inside the house.

The Pope is Gay

"It's not ridiculous. I'm telling you the Pope is gay!"

The woman, muscular as a female tennis pro, wore a plain black dress, black gloves, and a white lace scarf wrapped around her neck; not the typical look in this Village hotel bar crammed with hip and hippie types. Two men were seated at the end of the bar: the younger one, thin and sad-eyed, shook his head; the older man, a burly off duty cop, glared at the woman.

"I was in the Vatican choir," she continued. "Sipping grappa one night after rehearsal, the lead tenor kissed the cross he wore around his neck, and swore it was true. 'Two timed by the Pope. The Pope for Christ sake!' Those are his exact words!"

The lady bartender laughed: "C'mon Roberta."

"It ain't funny," the cop scowled.

"Hey, you're off duty, John. Don't take things so serious."

Roberta turned to him, smiled, and lifted her glass: "To peace and fun."

She downed her drink, took a bill out of her purse and put it on the bar.

"Time for Cinderella to leave the party." She winked at the bartender: "Next week."

She fluttered her eyes at the cop, and walked out of the bar.

"Cunt," he muttered loud enough for her to hear. He threw down a bill and got up to leave.

"She's a he," the bartender informed him.

The muscles in the cop's jaws tightened: "Cocksucker. Fags think everyone important is one of them. Like the Jews."

"He's not gay either," the bartender said. "Got a wife and kid."

"I heard about freaks like that in 'Nam," the other man said.

Roberta sat in the hotel lobby under a large poster of Fred Astaire in a classic ballroom pose with his sister. His real name was Robert, and he checked his watch. He didn't want to be on the street at night the times he cross dressed, so he always booked a car to drive him home; it was due any minute. With the masquerade about to end there was a twinge of sadness, like saying good-bye to someone you weren't sure you'd see again.

He looked up at the poster, and closed his eyes.

The cruise on the Queen Mary was his parents' anniversary present to themselves. The first night out at sea he was on the promenade deck staring down at the ocean, when a girl came and stood beside him. She seemed friendly, but he was too shy to start a conversation. She said they were so high up it was like flying over a lake. He'd never been in an airplane, but her father was a Congressman from Wisconsin, so she knew about planes and lakes.

He once heard his mother tell his father never to ask a woman her age, so he could only guess that she was sixteen, which would make her a year older than him. Her name was Arlene, her passion was poetry. She recited a famous poem about the sea, the one about the boy standing on a burning deck. It had something to do with death, and was written by a woman he never heard of.

The next day she read him one of her own poems, about a young girl who found a wounded bird and nursed it back to freedom. He told her he liked hers better than the other one. He was good at drawing and made one to illustrate her poem. She kissed him when he gave it to her.

A costume ball was scheduled for the last night at sea. She had an idea: they were the same size, he should come as a girl, she'd be a man. She coaxed him until he finally agreed. They came as a dance team and won second prize, a silver charm in the shape of the ship.

Robert smiled. He still had that charm.

The young man who was at the bar spotted Robert in the lobby; after what he'd heard, he was curious as hell to see her up close. He didn't want to be caught staring, so he pretended to be studying a photograph of Gloria Swanson.

"She was married to Wallace Beery."

He turned, it was her. Him. He should have known from the voice.

"Beery was a well known female impersonator."

"Is that what you are?"

"Did you figure it out yourself?" It was always a disappointment when someone did.

"The bartender told us. Shouldn't she?"

Roberta shrugged: "A female impersonator is a performer. He could be gay he could be straight. He could be a transvestite. The greatest in history was the Emperor Heliogabalus, the best of modern times was Julian Eltinge. Paramount starred him in 1917, in *The Clever Mrs. Carfax.* But I haven't answered your question. Men like me are cross-dressers. We like to dress up like women."

"Why?"

"A nod to all the daredevils who live the life they love." She reached in her purse and took out a faded newspaper clipping. "I keep this with me, sometimes I need to bolster my courage. It's a Winchell column from last year. I'll read it to you. *Neil Cargile, the Nashville tycoon, lunched yesterday with his girlfriend at the Tavern-on-the-Green. Cargile, 60, and reputed to be one of the ten richest men in America, made a grand entrance wearing a blazer, an open shirt, striped miniskirt, pantyhose and heels. This reporter approached his table and asked him Why. His answer was Cross dressing is fun!*"

The young man couldn't help but smile. The guy seemed happy with who he was which was more than he could say about himself. He put out his hand; the grip he received was a lot firmer than he'd expected.

"Well, nice to have met you."

He meant it and walked away.

Robert checked his watch again, shook his head, and thought 'there's always the subway.'

It wasn't much of a demonstration, but it was loud and intimidating. The organizer, Reverend Fred Phelps, was America's most rabid and vicious hater of homosexuals. A self described Baptist preacher, he wore a Texas Stetson and a long black coat, and held a placard high in the air. The photograph in the center was of Matthew Shepard, the gay University of Washington student who was savagely murdered because of his sexual orientation. His body hung over a barbed wire fence. Large red letters spelled out MATT IN HELL.

The Reverend's voice boomed out to the curious on-lookers:

"Thou shalt not lie with mankind as with womankind: it is abomination. Leviticus 18:22."

Robert would have crossed over to the other side of the street, but they were outside the entrance to the subway and there was no way to avoid them. He thought he recognized the burly cop from the bar, and smiled nervously at him. He got no response and figured it was his eyesight, not too good at night without his glasses; they spoiled the effect when he dressed up.

Someone handed him a pamphlet that read FAGS OUT OF OUR CITY. It was like holding a hot plate, but he thought the burly demonstrator was watching him so he put it in his purse and headed quickly for the subway entrance.

Half way down the stairs he heard someone following him. He turned around, there was no one there. His heart was beating too fast, a warning sign, the doctor told him after that last episode. It's those movies I've been seeing. No more. He took three deep breaths and felt a little better, any more would have made him light-headed.

The subway car was half full. He was still a little edgy and avoided eye contact with any of the riders, a basic rule he'd learned for keeping out of trouble. At the next stop a really tall black woman got on, with her a child who could barely reach up to her mother's hand. They sat down opposite him. He smiled at the little girl and she smiled back. He tried to imagine why they were out at night, where they were from, where they were going.

How old was I when mother dressed me up and took me with her when she went to lunch with friends. Four? Five maybe. What a beautiful child! How many times did they think I was a girl. I wanted to hide, but I never cried. Even when kids laughed at me and yelled Sissy! Sissy! Father brought home a punching bag and boxing gloves. No more drawing until I see you punch this bag like you really mean it!

The mother and child were gone, the train had passed his station. He got off, had to climb up to the exit level, cross over and come down on the other side to catch the car going back. Someone was behind him again. But it was ridiculous to turn around and look; did he expect to be alone in a New York subway station?

Prospect Park was Brooklyn's version of Central Park: pedestrian paths traversed wooded acreage and exited near apartment buildings that bordered the area. Robert lived in one of them. Across the street from the park entrance was a White Tower. His wife liked the donuts they made right on the premises; he'd bring some home for her.

It was a twenty minute walk around the park to his apartment, if he cut through the park he'd be home in ten, the donuts would still be warm. He'd never walked there after dark, and hesitated at the entrance. An archway framed the trees and foliage much like the view-finder in a camera: light from a lamp post created an effect that reminded him how years ago, in the museum not too far away, he tried to copy a moody Corot landscape.

An older couple sat on the first bench inside the park; they were holding hands, something he hadn't ever seen his parents do. They looked up at him and smiled. A silhouette in the distance choreographed a private embrace; overhead a star was cradled in a crescent moon. It was a beautiful night, perfect for a leisurely walk and daydreaming, something Robert liked to do to protect precious memories from fading away. Use it or lose it.

He finally decided to do something he had secretly dreamed about, dress like a woman. The first problem was not knowing anything about cosmetics, dress sizes, bra sizes, any of the skills women are required to master. He rented a 'how-to' cosmetics video put out by Revlon, and bought the current editions of Harper's Bazaar and Vogue to get an idea of what would look good on a five foot ten inch one hundred and forty pound woman. What he saw were outlandish clothes fit for a fancy costume party; he wanted to look like an average woman.

Too embarrassed to go into a store, he picked up a Sears and Roebuck catalogue. In the Big Girl section, a size chart helped him figure out what was needed. He selected a pink sweater, a wide pink belt, a white lace bra, a three pack of lace-trimmed panties, a white full slip, pantyhose, and a pair of high heeled shoes.

When everything arrived, he showered, and shaved closer than ever before. He stepped into the white panties and slid the pantyhose over them. They felt wonderful and he was engulfed in a warm feeling, only sorry he had waited so long; he couldn't believe what he'd been missing. He strapped himself into the white lace bra. It was tight but it felt good. He stuffed the cups with pantyhose then glided into the silky full slip.

An ambulance siren broke his mood. He always hated that sound, the images of suffering it conjured up. He looked around him. He hadn't realized how dark it was, and as the siren faded in the distance, how quiet. The only light came from a building not close enough for him to identify, the only sounds the faint hum of traffic. He had an instinct to take a path that led out of the park, but the need to finish his reverie took precedence.

He trembled when he put on the makeup, and had trouble follow-ing the instructions in the video: first the base, then the powder, blush, eyeliner, and lipstick. He used to watch his mother get ready to go out for an evening; she would sit in her slip with a drink and cigarette. 'Like mother, like son,' he thought, and did the same.

He looked in the mirror: something wasn't right. The hair. He was missing a wig. He wanted to look as much like a woman as he could the first time he dressed up, so he took everything off.

The next day he went down to the Village, bought a blond wig, and hurried back to the apartment for the big event. He slipped into his underthings just as he had the night before, placed a scarf over his face the way his mother did, then put on the wig. He felt bubbly and euphoric, almost drunk. The pink sweater dress fit loosely, he belted it with the pink belt, and slipped on the high heels. He was in heaven and couldn't tear himself away from the full length mirror on the closet door. He looked just like a woman. The complete calm when he saw himself transformed was like resting after a strenuous workout; the demands of manliness no longer threatened.

He stayed dressed for four hours; by then it was close to midnight and he had to leave for work early in the morning. Sadly he undressed and showered. He tried to sleep but images of the reflection in the mirror kept going through his head. He got up and put the panties back on, along with the bra and slip. When he went back to bed he slept like a baby.

Footsteps jarred him once again back to reality. His heart began to race. He tried to force himself to remain calm: this wasn't a movie, he was in a public park in a civilized city! The footsteps grew louder; someone was coming up behind him. He turned sharply. The jogger waved as he passed him by.

Idiot! Robert meant himself. He could see his apartment building now. Just three floors higher up and his own unit would be visible, but the cost of the park view from the upper levels was more than they could afford. Things were going to be better soon, he was sure of that. His boss at the ad agency promised to throw some of their business to him when he opened his own lab. To-morrow he'd be checking out two lofts in Soho.

"I was getting worried," his wife said, arranging the donuts on a plate. "I'll put up some decaf."

Robert took off his gloves and scarf.

"Car didn't show."

"Good time?"

"Enjoyable."

He removed the wig, and put it on a head mannequin.

"I'm thinking I'll change things next time, maybe be an ex-rabbi. The Pope's Jewish."

When in Rome

He counted forty-two tombstones. Jeff always counted things, even when he was a kid: the number of people in line waiting to get into a theater, how many boards there were across the boardwalk in Atlantic City. Knowing 'how many' meant one less thing open to question. His father was just the opposite: he hated to have anything pinned down. In baseball parlance you'd call him a free swinger.

The army shrink told Jeff that one way to take the focus off memories that were haunting him would be to think about things further in the past. He was willing to try anything, so here he was in the cemetery his father's mother and father were buried in.

The graveyard was behind the Trinity Church, a block south of Wall Street. The skyscraper was a little further on. It was still hard to believe that anyone could, would, be desperate enough to jump from sixty stories up, but his grandfather was one of those who had, brokers who lost everything in the Crash. The next day, unable to face the humiliation of poverty, his grandmother swallowed a bottle of sleeping pills.

His father never spoke about them, how he found out what happened, what he did afterwards; it was as though he had no memory of the events. But every year around the anniversary of Bloody Tuesday, Jeff knew to stay clear of him. It was the only time his father ever hit him. At night he'd hear him pacing his room and talking as though there was someone with him. After a while his father would lock his door, get into bed and stay there until the storm moved on, sometimes for a full day and night. Afterwards he was like a wind-locked sailboat, helplessly adrift. It was spooky.

Six months ago his father moved to Seabrook, Texas, still chasing the jackpot that had so far eluded him. It wasn't much of a detour on Jeff's bus trip back to LA. He called to let him know he was coming. It was no surprise that a woman answered the phone. There'd been plenty of them since the divorce, he wasn't sure about before. This one's name was Gloria.

"George's down at the dock. Your room's ready."

"Vets have funny habits. It might be better if I stayed at a motel."

"Your father will be disappointed."

"We'll have plenty of time."

"Your dime. The bus stops right outside Sonny's Bayview. Call when you get in. He'll pick you up."

That was one thing he'd done—picked him up from school after his mother was no longer around. They never talked much even then. Sometimes Jeff blamed himself—it wasn't all his father's fault the family broke up; sometimes he thought his father didn't like him—love was a word not often used in the house. Later he decided his father just wasn't able to put his feelings on display; the times he would try—touching a shoulder, a spontaneous kiss (usually on the top of the head)— his father's eyes would light up, but then he'd come up with some excuse that got him out of the room. It wasn't hard for Jeff to understand—it hit close to home.

Except for the black man across the aisle, he had the last row of the bus to himself. He stared out the window, conscious of neither time nor distance. The first rest stop, a roadhouse cafe in Pennsylvania, was crowded and there was a wait to get seated. The man who sat across the aisle put a dime in the newspaper dispenser, took out a copy of the Philadelphia Inquirer, and held the lid open. Jeff took a copy and muttered "Thanks."

"Can you believe this? A guy in Minnesota is suing the government for half a million bucks because treatment in a VA hospital changed his skin from black to white. Me . . . I'd pay the government."

"They can mess you up more ways than you can count," Jeff replied.

The black man got off in Birmingham, Alabama. Even though they hadn't spoken again, Jeff was sorry to see him go.

It started to pour, rain beating so hard on the roof, a believer would insist God was angry. In the jungle it came down like that as regular as Tuesday followed Monday, except the days of the week no longer had names. Hardly anybody in the platoon got to sleep until the monsoons stopped. All you could hear then were the left over raindrops falling to the ground from drenched leaves. The soothing sounds relieved tension that had built up during the day, and some of the men started to giggle. That's when he first spoke to the black corporal. He was from someplace in Alabama, the bus could be going right past it. Jeff never said good-bye to him either. A snapshot of the corporal's girlfriend was the only thing left intact after the AK got through tattooing his body. She probably married some guy smart enough to stay out of the army. The way Margo did.

Sonny's Bayview Motel was at the far end of the one block long Main Street. To get to it the bus passed the general store, a unisex hair parlor, a cafe with a plate of giant ribs in the window, a liquor store, and an unenclosed public telephone that stood like a lone sentry watching over the town. Jeff felt like he was on the back lot of a film studio.

The motel itself had a certain charm, most of the rooms, as promised, with a view of the bay. He rang the bell on the counter. The man who sauntered out from the back was six feet tall with a pot belly so big his belt couldn't reach around it and hung a foot below. It wasn't high season—Seabrook, known as the capitol of Galveston Bay, was popular with Texans who came down for boating and fishing in the summer when you could barely breathe the humid air in the cities. Jeff took the special offer, three nights for the price of two. The bargain room overlooked the parking lot.

It was close to sundown and he thought he'd watch the sunset before he called his father. He and Margo would sometimes drive to Malibu where if you were lucky the sky would end up looking like a French Impressionist painting. A maid's cart blocked the narrow walkway. When he started to move it she rushed out of the room next door, and pushed it to one side.

"Sorry mister."

The face of an innocent, the body of a temptress, the same green eyes as Margo, one eyebrow arched higher than the other. That was a shitty decision he made, coming to New York to see her right out of the hospital. It was going to take time to get her out of his mind. She liked to tell how when she was only fourteen, boys whistled when she passed by. The maid was probably not much older than that. Sensing that he was staring at her, she posed for a moment like she was having her picture taken, then wheeled the cart into a storage room at the end of the corridor.

She was out in a flash, and with two fingers in her mouth, whistled with the authority of a sergeant signaling roll call. Jeff had tried doing it but what came out sounded like he was blowing away a feather. A dog came out from behind a clump of bushes. Jeff had never seen such a funny looking animal, gray whiskers, bone skinny, one foreleg bent outwards like it was pointing at something. Its tail wagged faster than its legs could move. The girl and her dog walked side by side down a dirt path until they were out of sight. Like the ending of a Chaplin movie.

His father got out of a Chevy pickup, and held out his hand:

"You look pretty good, considering."

"You too dad."

It wasn't true. He'd always stood tall, (with the help of elevator shoes), and when he walked, swaggered like he had everything under control. Now all the bravado seemed leached out of him. The truck too had seen better days.

Past the liquor store the road headed down to the bay, and pretty soon a row of commercial fishing boats came into view. The Chevy pulled up alongside one of them.

"This is it. I own fifty per cent." He pointed to the name painted on the hull: "Daisy's my partner's live in. On the starboard side . . . this side's port . . . it says 'Gloria.' You talked to her on the phone."

Jeff wasn't sure if his father was proud or embarrassed. He stared at the three flags that hung from the back of the boat: the Stars and Stripes, Texas, and the Confederacy. "You've got all the bases covered."

"They take their patriotism serious down here. A good thing to keep in mind. And they love you vets."

He backed the pickup away from the dock.

"You and Gloria living together long?" Jeff asked, trying to get a conversation going.

"A while. It was lonesome before I met her, not knowing anybody."

Pretty soon the road curved, and there in front of them could have been Ran Se, or Tra Bong, or My Khe: tiny hootches bunched close together like puppies trying to keep warm. Jeff thought he'd seen the last of them.

"No good nosying around here at night," his father said, and stepped on the gas.

"Around town they call it Little Saigon. They came here thinking they'd be slaughtered by the commies after we pulled out."

Jeff nodded. An intelligence officer in the ward bragged about how we planted that idea, to disrupt Vietnam's transition to independence.

The house was at the other end of the bay, in the middle of a row of about twenty others, all pretty much the same: modest and weather beaten like the boats. Gloria fit in like she'd come with the house. Not good looking or bad, her hair was coifed almost a foot high, which made her taller than his father. On first glance Jeff thought she was twenty years his junior, but when light penetrated the makeup, he could see the tell-tale markers of her age.

She had spent all her life in this small town, knew every man woman and child in it, and like most of them, wasn't comfortable with strangers, particularly the northern variety. The drink before dinner helped loosen things up a bit. She told about her husband and teenage son still lying in their muddy grave under thirty feet of water:

"The fishing was good. They stayed out until it was too late to beat the storm." She was an operator in the local beauty parlor, which is where his father met her.

"Funny at first, having my hair cut by a woman," he said. "Now I like it."

Not surprisingly dinner was fish, which Gloria prepared as simply as if they were out camping. She served the same way. The more they talked the more she reminded him of his mother, which was odd because his mother would have prepared and served the meal according to rules laid out in Good Housekeeping. This lady had rules of her own that she played by. However different, you could bet both women would defend what they believed in the way a lioness protects her cubs. It was a good idea to watch what you said and did to both of them.

Jeff's father told about how he'd seen the ad in *Money* magazine, and decided to buy into the boat.

"Not before I researched the business."

"So what's involved in catching enough shrimp to make the venture pay off?" Jeff asked.

"Get the boat to the right place, drop a net and drag it over the bottom. That's it. The Japanese think they're great for a hard on . . . can't buy enough of them. Tom, my partner, has been raking in the dough."

"Why'd he sell you half?"

"Capitalism. Had his eye on a second boat. Only problem there's just so many shrimp out there and now there's competition."

"Ya'all better hit the sack early," Gloria said. "You're going out before the cock wakes up."

Jeff's father nodded and got up:

"I'll take you back to the motel."

"What's with getting up so early?" Jeff asked when they were in the pickup.

"Tom wants to show off in front of a war hero. "

"I hate that. I never said I was a hero."

Four in the morning, the shore of Galveston Bay felt a lot like the Botangang Peninsula: you couldn't see much beyond your own hand, ghostly echoes bounced off the water. Tom wore a short-sleeved T-shirt, exposing arms that could pass for a wall display in a tattoo parlor. He introduced Jeff to two men who were getting ready to board the boat.

"My partner's boy. He was over there fighting the little bastards."

Jeff pegged the burly one an over-the-hill wrestler, the other, skinny, with a face pockmarked like a field hit by mortar fire, was called 'Preacher.'

"You're in for a treat," Preacher said. "Comes a time to grab the bull by the nuts. Years back some men put on Indian clothes, dumped some tea overboard, and that's how this country came about."

Tom handed his father a rifle, then held one out to Jeff. He'd had enough of guns, and hesitated taking it. Tom seemed annoyed that he had to explain.

"We've had rules here go back fifty or more years. Civilized rules. The trouble is the squinty-eyes ain't civilized, don't give a shit about rules. Sneak their boats into whatever area we're working. If we don't drive them out we'll end up in the crapper."

"It would be a helluva lot better to talk to them, we were the ones gave up," Jeff told his father as they climbed into the boat.

It might have meant something if he'd told it to Tom, but Jeff shied away from confrontation when he wasn't sure about the outcome. That was how he lost Margo. When he got the draft notice she told him not to go. 'Are you willing to die for a war that is immoral and illegal?' He didn't have the guts to take a stand.

They pushed away from the dock without starting the engine, and drifted silently with the tide. It was as quiet as if a casket was being lowered into the ground. By the time the first rays of the sun appeared on the horizon, they were within sight of the docked Vietnamese boats.

The engine fired up, the boat lurched towards the unsuspecting village, picking up speed as it got closer. Preacher and the wrestler came up from the hold carrying five gallon cans of gasoline. When it seemed the boat would ram one of the tied up vessels, Tom swerved it 180 degrees, the two hulls almost touching. The gasoline was dumped over the other boat's deck, Tom tossed in a lit torch, and the Vietnamese skiff burst into flames. He whooped and fired his gun in the air; Preacher and the wrestler followed suit. Jeff turned his back and went down into the hold. It took only a moment for his father to make his choice: he didn't fire his gun, but he cheered.

When the boat docked they all climbed out. Jeff was propping his gun against the side of the hull when a hand clamped hard onto his shoulder. He spun around, it was Tom.

"Too bad you didn't like the show." His voice sounded sweet, but with the bitterness of artificial sweetener. "Mind your P's and Q's, soldier boy."

Jeff was glad when the pickup pulled away from the dock.

"Your partner's a loose cannon."

"Don't underestimate him. He's head of the local Klan."

"The KKK?"

"The same."

"I thought that went out years ago."

"Believe me they're for real. They let everybody know you're either with them or you're their enemy. Understand what I'm telling you?"

Jeff did. He was brought up not to look for trouble.

His father opened the door to the house like he was sneaking in.

"Gloria sleeps late on her day off."

He turned on the coffee maker.

"I don't remember . . . cream and sugar?"

Jeff shook his head.

"Did you know what they were going to do?"

"They just want to put a little scare into those people."

"Your friends aren't going to be satisfied with just scaring them."

"Tom's a family man. Coaches Little League. Look . . . two or three good catches I can bail out with a profit. Until then, well you know the expression, 'when in Rome. . . .' Anyway I'm not really the one responsible."

"If anybody gets hurt, killed is more likely, you're as guilty as the others. Call the police while there's still time."

"Most of them are Klan too. Gloria told me."

"Then let the FBI know. They'll have an office in Galveston."

"I'm not cut out for a whistle blower." He put his hand on Jeff's arm: "We been up since three, we can both use some shuteye. What do you say? There's an extra room right down the hall."

Jeff nodded. He watched his father tip-toe into the bedroom.

Gloria hung up the phone when he walked in.

"I thought you were sleeping."

"The phone woke me up. Wrong number."

He nodded: "Happened to me the other day. The boy's in the other room."

"I know," she said and headed for the bathroom.

He should have been more careful talking to Jeff. Women were like cats that can hear a mouse breathing behind a brick wall. He called after her:

"He's a smart kid. Won't make any trouble."

Jeff lay on his back with his eyes open, staring at the ceiling. There was no denying he had a lot in common with his father. They both believed what they wanted to believe. In the jungle, when the unit celebrated a victory, Jeff saw fools, the happy ending was mere illusion. When others were pissing their pants afraid of dying, he could convince himself the danger didn't apply to him, it wasn't his time. Time was what defined his survival, controlled his destiny. He knew now that it was time for him to move on. It was no good his being here, for him or his father. It would be a relief for both of them to have one less unpleasant truth to face.

Gloria was in the kitchen sipping a mug of coffee.

"Can I borrow the pickup to go to the motel? I've got a call to make."

"That's a phone right in front of you."

"The number's in my backpack."

She studied him a moment, then picked up the keys.

"I'll take you."

The maid was making up the bed when Jeff walked into the room. He said "Hi" and started rifling through his backpack.

"You remind me of a girlfriend I once had. She married another guy."

He took his address book and a bus schedule out of the backpack, and zipped it back up.

"That's a cute dog you've got, by the way."

"You can say funny looking, Mister. We don't mind."

Jeff smiled. She had Margo's attitude too. He walked out of the room and headed for the front desk. When he got there Gloria was talking to the room clerk like they had a secret between them.

"Something's come up, I have to leave early," he told the clerk. Can I get back the extra day I paid for?"

"Bud can arrange it," Gloria said.

He nodded: "See me when you check out," he told Jeff.

"You wouldn't happen to have the bus schedule to Galveston."

Bud pointed to a rack near the door that held postcards and ads for boat rentals.

His father was up when they returned.

"Your boy's leaving for Galveston," Gloria told him, and went into the bedroom.

"It's time I got home," Jeff explained. "Maybe I can get my old job back. The agency told me to let them know when I got out. Okay if I call from here?"

His father pushed the phone over, Jeff picked up the receiver.

"Soon's she gets off."

He put the local and the cross country bus schedules on the table. It took a while to figure them out.

"There's one to Galveston at three. I can make the five o'clock to the Coast."

Gloria came back out of the bedroom. She pecked his father on the cheek:

"You two can have some family time. I'll have the truck back."

"Good or bad," his father asked when Jeff got off his call.

"Flip a coin. Heads, they knew who I was . . . tails, they'll see what can be done." He shrugged. "There's no guarantee. Even with heads, you can lose."

"Think positive."

"Want to know what I think? I think you should get out of here. You have nothing in common with these people . . . they aren't your friends. Come back to L.A. with me. Forget the money."

"Lose everything? You still haven't learned the basics of life."

"Maybe you're right about that. Me telling you what to do, I can't get things right for myself."

"Your war's behind you at least."

Jeff shook his head: "Death is chasing me like a bounty hunter. It toys with me. In the hospital we were three to a room. The GI in the bed to my left moaned all the time. One day he cries out he can't breath and he's dying, but in a week he's kissing his girlfriend and walks out of the hospital. In the other bed was a sergeant from Louisiana. He never complained. Sunday he comes back from chapel, chipper and still singing something about Jesus. The next day he's wheeled out feet first. But you're a survivor, dad. You've hit the canvas before and bounced right back up."

"Don't think I haven't thought about walking away from this deal. But you need to know when to take yourself out of the game. It's too late for me to start over again."

He put his hand lightly on his son's arm, then, with a shyness reserved usually for the very young, embraced him. For a brief moment the intimacy held them captive, but it was too late for feelings so long neglected, to take root. They pulled back from one another, embarrassed.

"Couple of hours before you have to go," Jeff's father said. There was no emotion in his voice. "You always liked the beach, we can go there if you like. It runs clear around the bay."

"Can you walk it to the motel?"

"I don't see why not."

"How long do you think it would take?"

"An hour or so I'd guess. Is that what you want to do?"

"I won't have much chance to stretch my legs for a while."

"I'll walk you to the beach."

Just outside the door, the sun reflected off a seashell that was in perfect condition. Jeff picked it up and put it in his pocket.

The maid was on her way to the linen room when she spotted the clerk coming out of one of the rooms. She couldn't tell exactly which one but she'd seen him sneak a girl inside before. She was afraid of him. Whenever he got close enough, his hand would brush against her breasts and he would laugh. She ducked inside until she was sure he was gone.

She was tired, and glad there were only a few more rooms to clean. She went by the one the nice young man stayed in, and saw that there was dirt under the door. She cleaned that room especially well, and she saw him leave the motel in a truck. It must have been where the clerk did his dirty business. It wouldn't take long to tidy it up.

Jeff hadn't yet come into sight of Main Street when he heard the explosion. By the time he reached the motel, police and firemen were all over the place. He explained he had a bus to catch and just wanted to get his bag, but it was no go. What the hell, everything he really needed was in the wallet he had with him. He'd call his father from the first stop. Gloria could get her friend Bud to send the backpack on to him.

A sound from the past, startled him. He turned and saw a body being wheeled out of the motel on a gurney. The crazy-looking dog, trying desperately to hang on to it with his one good leg, was whining like that Vietnamese woman whose picture he'd taken holding a dead child in her arms. The C.O. said it wasn't what the Pentagon was looking to hand out to the media and tore it up.

He sat down on the bench at the bus stop. He wasn't aware that he was crying, until a man's voice asked if he was all right.

"Someone in there you knew?"

Jeff looked up. The man looked a little like the strange, old Indian who kept popping up in his dreams.

"No. I don't know anyone here."

Hard as he tried he couldn't figure out why he'd broken down the way he did. It couldn't have been the girl; he was sorry for what happened to her but no more than that. Margo was beyond crying about. It would be comforting if he could believe it had to do with his father, but he felt only pity and regret when he thought about him.

Maybe it was that Post something-or-other Syndrome the intern told him he had. Christ knows there was plenty to cry about, but he hadn't shed one tear the whole time there. It wasn't that he never cried—he was always self conscious about the way he teared up at the movies— but there was a good reason he couldn't in Vietnam. The women, the old men, the children, they never cried when their villages were littered with corpses, never called out in pain, even after a grenade tore a limb off their bodies. Not ever, when one of us could see or hear them.

Maybe he was just crying for himself.

The movement of the bus was soothing, almost like being rocked in a cradle. The overhead lights were turned off. He put the seat back as far as it would go, and closed his eyes.

The bus driver's voice beamed out over the speaker, and startled him:

"Say good-bye to Texas, folks! We've crossed into New Mexico."

Kit Carson! Billy the Kid!

How many pioneers had followed the great frontier scout on this road when it was only a dirt trail? How many times had Billy the Kid ridden it to escape the law? It never mattered to Jeff that the stories might have been made up.

Gunshots shattered his reverie. For a brief moment lightning lit up the pitch black sky. Billy the Kid was firing his gun in the air and laughing at the posse chasing him.

It got dark again. Jeff cried out:

"Turn on the lights!"

Masquerade

1

Caught twice and sent back by the Border Patrol, Roberto was sixteen when he finally made it from Guadeloupe to Riverside, California, the last address the family had for his father who had gone to America to earn the money for a small farm.

He washed windshields, picked grapes and strawberries, apricots and cotton, dug ditches, poured cement, unloaded fifty pound sacks of feed and fertilizer. Wherever he worked he showed the photograph his father had taken at a traveling fair that stopped at the village one year. Most people shook their heads, one said he saw him fall when goons charged into a line of union pickets, another remembered seeing him escape into the corn fields during the violence. A woman searching for her missing son thought she saw him in the morgue, but the face had been badly beaten and she couldn't be sure.

The authorities looked the other way when cheap, illegal labor was needed, so Roberto stayed close to wherever he was working. Hunger persuaded him to gamble that he would be safe at the festival *Acion de Gracias*, held every year in Catholic Churches throughout the area. People brought what they could to give thanks to god: a chicken, an armful of corn, a sack of wheat, home-made delicacies. Everyone was welcome; there would be crowds, he'd be a pebble in a field of corn.

The slim, dark-haired girl handing out tamales, was about his age. Her hands bore the calluses of hard work.

"They're made with blue corn. It only grows in the summer."

"Gracias."

"You can come back for another one if you like it."

Her smile was easy and friendly; her name was Esperanza. Although she worked in the fields, she was a citizen of the United States. Her father, a third generation Latino, disappeared after the union accused him of informing for the growers. Her mother, unable to face raising a child by herself, deposited the three year old at a cousin's house. It was believed she joined her husband somewhere far away.

When he was eighteen, Roberto gave up the search for his father, and married Esperanza. Hoping to find a better life in the big city, they moved to Los Angeles. Esperanza found work cleaning the homes of the rich; Roberto waited long and patiently on sidewalks scattered throughout the city, where people came seeking illegals who asked no questions and did menial work others shunned. More than once he was taken outside the city, worked ten or eleven hours, then was stranded without being paid.

When he understood enough English he got a job at the Bel Air Country Club. He set poison and disposed of rats that infested the property, laid sprinkler pipes, cleaned the sand traps and mowed the greens on the golf course. He never saw himself as exploited or underpaid, and accepted as natural that the only people of color seen on the grounds were the gardening and cleanup crews; even the caddies were white. When he became assistant to the supervisor of the grounds crew, he saw to it that those beneath him strictly obeyed the club's codes of behavior and dress.

2

After two miscarriages, Esperanza gave birth to a daughter they named Maria. Consumed by the demands of mere survival, there was little time to supervise the joyous, exuberant child. In the second grade she was given the IQ test. Spanish being the preferred language at home, Maria was less than fluent in English, and unfamiliar with the nuances of Anglo culture important in understanding the questions. She scored low on the test, and was labeled a slow learner. It would mark her permanently, as surely as the brand on a concentration camp inmate's arm.

She grew taller than her parents, had the grace and figure of an artist's model, green eyes shaped in the manner of a cat's. Believing that she was of lesser worth than the other students, Maria was like a coin tossed in the air, unpredictable which side would turn up: one side moody and confrontational; the other enthusiastic and cheerful; one stubborn; the other a willing follower; one Maria unrealistically upbeat; the other bitter in the belief she was doomed to a lifetime of shit work.

As immigrants find their countrymen, so Maria fell in with other troubled juveniles. The current badge of honor among many of them, an act that proved they were fearless, beyond the pale, was 'cutting,' a self mutilation not dissimilar from what penitents the world over use to prove their dedication to the faith. Maria was introduced to the practice in the girls' restroom.

Her friend held a paper clip, bent open to function as a scalpel, poised over her forearm. She began to laugh, a humorless sound a discerning adult would recognize as a cry for help. She squeezed her eyes shut, and brought her hand down sharply. The dull edge of the paper clip ripped open a jagged gash; blood dripped onto the floor. She wiped the tears from her eyes, undid the bandanna she wore around her forehead, and tied it around the wound. For the moment, the pain of the wound obliterated the deeper pain she couldn't talk about. There was added satisfaction doing it in school. She flipped her finger defiantly, thumbing her nose at one of her tormentors.

"It didn't hurt."

"I couldn't do it," Maria said.

"You can. You will."

Some kids joined gangs, some drank or smoked when others did, some took drugs; peer pressure the professionals call it. Maria cut.

3

Is it all right if I come in different faces?
No one will know who I am.
I'll hide behind the fish tank.
Everything is fuzzy
looking through the water.
Would you mind if I was you
for a while?

The English teacher found it scribbled on the back of a book report Maria turned in.

"Did you write this?"

"I forgot it was there."

"Have you written any others?"

Maria shrugged. "Some."

"I'd like you to bring them in."

"Why?"

"It will be your assignment for creative writing."

Maria thought why not? Easier than doing homework.

"Okay."

"You don't like school do you?"

She shrugged again, her patented, safe, non-response.

"Albert Einstein didn't do well in school," the teacher offered.

"I hate math."

Most of the teachers assigned to schools in the barrio, feel threatened and do what they can to get transferred out. Not Lilian Roth. She'd been there for years, and thrived on the challenge of reaching teenagers who had given up on themselves. She gave Maria a slim volume of poetry written by women. It came as a revelation that there were famous women poets. She read most of them; Emily Dickinson was her favorite.

The notice from the school district came the week before the semester ended. It was signed by the principal.

. . . .*President Bush's Education Reform* . . . *Tests to monitor reading, mathematics, and science* . . . *Budget cuts* . . . *Art, creative writing, dropped from the curriculum.* . . .

Maria shrugged. Nothing good ever lasted. Nobody was going to know she gave a damn!

Saturdays she went to the movies with friends. The theater was only a few blocks from home, in the Alvarado district not far from downtown L.A. People working in the big office buildings came there for lunch. 'It's like being in Mexico only better because it's safe to drink the water.' *Paychecks Cashed,* and *Loans,* signs all over the place weren't meant for them but for the locals who shopped in the mom and pop stores where you needed a Berlitz if you didn't read or speak Spanish.

It used to be an upscale neighborhood, and bordered a park that was once popular with families who took their kids rowing on the man-made lake. Now the park was a haven for the homeless, the lake polluted and abandoned even by the ducks who used to feast on bread crumbs and crackers tossed to them by the children. There were always cops around, watching to see if the homeless were dealing drugs, which Maria thought was pretty dumb because if they did they wouldn't have to sleep on the ground.

After the film, Maria and her friend went to the neighborhood version of Starbucks, then parted ways. Maria decided to take a short cut through the park. Men and women were sleeping on the hard ground, frightened children stared blankly out at the world. She felt an overpowering sadness, and anger that there wasn't anything she could do about it.

At the far end of the lake a woman about her mother's age, caught her attention. She was putting something into a wire cage. She looked up when Maria got close.

"We're trying to control the population of a colony of feral cats that live in the area," she explained.

"Do you put them to sleep?"

"No, no. I take them to a veterinarian close by. He neuters them and cuts a little nick in one ear so I don't bring the same ones back."

"Cool. When do you come back to see if you caught one?"

"I don't leave. If they're in the cage too long they hurt themselves trying to get out. If I don't get one in half an hour I'll try again Tuesday."

"Okay if I hang around? I'll be quiet."

They walked over to a bench nearby, and sat down, their eyes focused on the trap.

"When I'm on my own I'm going to get a dog. Maybe a cat later," Maria said "Ever get a kitten?"

The woman nodded: "It's different with them. I find someone to work with them, then they're put out for adoption. They can become wonderful pets, but it takes a lot of patience. And love."

"Doing what?"

"You start off sitting in a small room with the kitten. They're terrified of everything unfamiliar so there can't be anything inside for it to climb on or hide behind. I sat for six hours my first day with Samson. That's what I named the fella' who's lived with me for three years now. I talked to him softly, like putting a baby to sleep. After three days I was able to touch him. The first time he let me pick him up I cried, I was so happy."

"Neat! School's out next week. Maybe you'll catch a kitten. I'm good with animals."

'Mom's a good person. Even though she's scared of cats, she let me use my bathroom to train the kitten. She says she was always afraid of them, that you can't tell what they're thinking when they look at you, they never come when you call them, they don't listen to anything you say. I guess she felt that way about me when I was little. Maybe she still does. She goes into the kitchen and closes the door when I bring him into the house. I knock to let her know I'm coming out.

'I guess I'm claustro. If I didn't have my diary to write in I'd go batty. He sits there staring at me. Never closes his eyes. People say I have cats eyes. My hair's black too, just like the kitten's fur, only he's got white feet and a white ring around his eyes. Like a Halloween mask.

'It's my third day. He's feral, let me tell you. A fighter. It's a good thing the lady told me to wear gloves. I decided he needs a name. I fiddled around with some ideas, 'Wild Thing' was the one that fit best. I touched him for the first time with the eraser at the end of my pencil, and kind of stroked him with it a while. Then I used my finger. When he let me hold him I got so excited I screamed as loud as I could. Mom thought I got hurt. She was pretty upset.'

The deal was it was okay having the cat in the house for a few days, as long as it was locked in the bathroom. But when you're sixteen, you don't pay much attention to what's been agreed to; it's all about what you want. Maria wanted to keep Wild Thing; her mother wouldn't let her.

"I wish you weren't my mother! I wish I were somebody else!"

4

Randolph White specialized in immigration law. A thirty-five year old bachelor, his practice was modest but he took challenging cases, and once appeared before the Supreme Court, where to most academics' surprise he won a verdict that granted rights previously denied to immigrants.

Wednesdays he lunched at Langers delicatessen. A relic from the past, when its patrons were of a different class, the pastrami was still considered by many, superior to New York's. The bus stopped in front of the building his office was in, it was only two stops to the barrio. He liked riding among the locals, not at all self-conscious at sometimes being the only Anglo aboard. After lunch he strolled the residential streets nearby.

The *For Sale* sign kept beckoning him back to a structure as out of place and time as the delicatessen. The mansion, its grounds covered with weeds, was an architectural masterpiece. The young Langer who now ran the deli, told Randolph that his father used to deliver platters of cold cuts for high stakes poker games hosted there by the owner, Charlie Chaplin. An influx of Latinos and blacks into the neighborhood, pushed the wealthy, west to Beverly Hills.

Randolph was possessed when the idea struck him. It took him three years to raise the money and get the necessary permits, but finally there emerged Casa Libre, or Freedom House as it's sometimes called, a refuge for twenty five homeless and illegal teenagers, taken off the streets. Most of them had sneaked across the border from Mexico with their parents' consent, dreaming of jobs and money to send home, only to sink into a quicksand of fear and despair, prey to the law, and to those driven by their own desperate circumstances to become hunters of the weak. At Casa Libre they would be registered in schools, have their medical needs tended to, trained for jobs and gotten green cards.

Lilian Ross was Randolph's resource when it came to testing and placing the residents in appropriate schools. It was she who suggested that the building behind the main house, built by Chaplin for guests, be turned into an Arts Center, open to the entire community.

"Mr. White liked the idea," she told Maria. "You can read whichever poem you choose."

"I never meant to read them out loud."

"That's what poets do."

Maria didn't respond.

"You'll be sharing your gift with the community. Others bring pottery they've made, drawings, photographs."

"Suppose they hate it."

"Not everyone will like what you've written. That's not important."

She stood on an improvised platform before twenty or thirty people, among them half a dozen residents of the main house. In front of her in the first row, a boy, slumped down in his seat, stared up at her. She stood erect, stared back at him defiantly, and looked out at the rest of the audience. If they didn't like her poetry tough shit!

"Subliminal messages
that I hear in the wind.
I look to my shooting
star, but you are dim,
dimmer as my dreams
get reeled in by your
hook. You baited me for
disaster, and throw me
down."

"Unravel the web
unspindle the twine, undo the
spell. Grant me the serenity."

"Wild heart

passionate to feel all
to save the world.
Green eyes loving any creature
or critter in need.
Tender Heart."

"Bright smile
Hi, I'm Sandra,
I slide down a rainbow,
land in a pot of gold."
"Lies!"

Mr. White was genuinely enthusiastic: "That was really good, Maria. Come back and read for us again."

She couldn't hold back a smile, and nodded.

"The poem seems to be your own voice," he said. "Why did you call yourself Sandra?"

"I don't like my name. Some day I'll change it."

"Maria's pretty."

"I don't believe the stories about her in the Bible."

"Okay. Sandra is short for Cassandra. You'll have the gift of prophecy. It's Greek mythology."

"I never got into mythology."

"I'll tell you about her. Apollo, second in power only to Zeus, fell in love with her, but that love was not returned. He promised that if she complied with his desires he would bestow on her the gift of prophecy. She accepted his proposal, received the gift, then refused his favors."

"What happened to her?"

"When Troy was invaded she was killed."

One of the residents caught his eye, he was waiting to talk to Maria.

"I'm hogging you," Mr. White told her. "Thanks for participating in the program."

It was the boy who sat in the front row. She was surprised that he was tall and good looking. Handsome, really.

"Saying 'lies' at the end, spoiled the poem."

"It's how I felt. Feel."

"You always say how you feel?"

"On paper."

He nodded: "It's still light out. I can show you our garden."

He took a few steps towards the exit, stopped and looked back at her. Maria followed him.

A dirt path bordered the low brick wall that circled behind the main house. It was an unusual night for downtown LA: bright moon, blue skies, you could even make out some stars. For a moment it looked like there was a shooting star, but it was only a plane on approach to nearby Burbank airport.

He pointed to a long row of plants: "Lettuce, peppers, tomatoes. You smell the fertilizer I put in this afternoon after school."

"What school do you go to?"

"Crenshaw High."

"Me too. How come I've never seen you?"

"I'm behind two grades. There wasn't much time for school where I came from." He sat down on the brick wall. "Sit a while."

She sat down near him: "Do you like it here?"

"It's okay. I'd rather be home."

"Why did you leave?"

"My mother couldn't feed all of us."

"It was something like that with my father. He came from Guadalupe when he was our age. All by himself."

Ramon hadn't told anyone about his own experience, but he hadn't met anyone as easy to talk to.

"Six of us started out. A coyote was supposed to lead us across the desert. The two-legged kind. They take your money and make promises they don't keep. Third day we heard a helicopter the border patrol uses. We hid in a ravine, and went to sleep. When we woke up the coyote was gone. With all our food and water. My cousin was the first one died."

Afraid of exposing emotions he'd been taught weren't manly, he stood up: "We've got curfew. They're pretty strict here."

Maria wanted to comfort him, but she didn't know how, and got up. They looked at one another a moment, then she started to leave.

"See ya . . ."

"Ever go to the Taco Stand on Alvarado for lunch?"

"Sure. I'll come to-morrow."

The centerpiece of conversation for Maria's girlfriends, was boys, flights of fancy about the number who vied for their attention. Maria soared to greater heights: she fell in love. As with everything she did her commitment was total; reality was blinded by the glare of her enthusiasm. She'd let him know how she felt, Saturday, after the movie. She'd write a poem, that would be the best way, kind of like an anniversary since it was the way they met.

She'd never written one about love before, so it didn't come easily. Maybe she'd get an idea or an inspiration from the book Miss Roth gave her. She sort of remembered one by Elizabeth Browning that hadn't really interested her, but she wasn't into thinking about love then.

Unless you can think, when the song is done,
No other is soft in the rhythm;
Unless you can feel when left by One,
That all men else go with him,
that your beauty itself wants proving;
Unless you can swear "For life, for death!"
Oh fear to call it loving.

Unless you can muse in a crowd all day.
On the absent face that fixed you;
Unless you can love as the angels may,
With the breath of heaven betwixt you;
Unless you can dream that his faith is fast,
Through behoving and unbehoving,
Unless you can die when the dream is past,
Oh never call it loving!

She didn't have to write anything; she'd memorize some of that poem.

They were in a corner of the park where they could feel like they were alone. Maria recited:

"Unless you can feel when left by One, that all men else go with him; unless you can swear For life, for death! Oh never call it loving!"

Ramon didn't say anything right away, and Maria couldn't wait: "Well?"

"I liked what you wrote better," Ramon said. "It was easier to understand."

The truth was he did understand: he understood that more was expected of him than he was willing to give. He had his own agenda, his own dreams: of being independent, making money, having lots of girls. He reached into his pocket and took out a sheet of bright yellow paper. Maria had seen flyers like it tacked on to vacant buildings in the neighborhood, sometimes in the restroom at school. Large red letters were superimposed over lurid drawings of naked women in provocative poses.

RAVE PARTY

SEX, DRUGS, ALCOHOL

"My friend gave me two tickets."

Maria hesitated.

" You don't have to come."

The entrance was through a vacant lot behind a warehouse. Smoke filled the cavernous space, Hard Rock blared out from a dozen speakers. The floor was so tightly packed, bodies were no longer in pairs, and formed a homogenous, writhing mass, arms flailing wildly, a thousand-tenacled monster poised to seize anything within reach. In one corner of the room, teenagers were inhaling nitrous oxide through balloons, others were making out under flashing lights.

Ramon came back from the bar, carrying two paper cups filled with beer. They hooked arms, drank from each other's cup, and kissed.

A girl not far from them screamed. Two boys started yelling, and a fight broke out. Then sounds familiar to most of the partygoers who lived in gang infested areas—gunshots. Pandemonium broke loose. Ramon grabbed her hand and pulled her through the mass of bodies heading desperately for the exit.

"Run!" he told her when they got to where you could see outside.

She made it out before the police arrived, but Ramon was trapped in the building. Three partygoers were dead: two boys, one girl. Ramon would be sent back to Mexico. She'd never see him again.

It was after midnight when she got home. She took off her shoes, went to the kitchen, took an empty pie tin out of a cabinet, tip-toed up the stairs, and went into the bathroom where her father kept his razor.

Blood dripped into the pie tin she placed under her dressing table. She looked up, saw her image in the mirror, and began to sob. Her notepad and pen were on the table. With one hand she pressed a tampon against the wound, with the other she wrote:

I'm crying out . . . help!
My arms are my proof.
Razors, nail files,
My cutting pleasures.
Somebody help me.
Push up my sleeves,
Take that knife,
Slice my arms,
Let my blood drip over the floor.

Why can't you see my sadness,
Only the comfort of scissors.
I can't put my sleeves down.
No one cares.

5

Esperanza framed a photograph of Maria in uniform, and kept it on the stand beside her bed. On Maria's dressing table she put the priest's blessing that likened joining the war in Iraq akin to serving god, and a bank book in Maria's name, that recorded the $15,000 bonus the government gave her to enlist in the army.

Roberto was immensely proud of his daughter. He bought an American flag, and hung it outside the house. Every evening he took it down and folded it the way they did at the country club; in the morning, when he put it back into its stand, his lips moved silently: "God bless America."

Whenever he could he carried his radio with him. Every hour, on the hour, he turned it on for news of Iraq. He never questioned that the war was necessary to protect America, that his daughter would return home a hero, having served her country proudly.

Maria was assigned to the Quartermaster Corps. Her original duties were clerical, inventorying incoming supplies, and tracking them as they were distributed from the supply depot in Baghdad. The job was too passive for her, and she volunteered for one of the most dangerous assignments in the army: delivering the supplies. Anything on or near every highway and byway in Iraq could be wired and lethal: a rock, garbage, a dead body, an animal, even a child.

The sixty inch, high-definition Sony Television set, complete with Satellite dish, was headed for Falouja. Maria was driving a Humvee that like most of the vehicles used to deliver supplies, had Band-Aids of scrap metal attached to the undercarriage by the drivers, desperate for some protection from the deadly explosives. There were all kinds of explanations as to why only a few came with proper armor, and promises that the situation would be rectified, but almost every day, some GI lost a limb or his life to bureaucracy, corruption, or just plain fucked up priorities.

The corporal who rode 'point' beside her in the front seat, was a National Guardsman from Mississippi. He was a black man but not much darker than Ramon. His eyes were sad like the blood hound's she sometimes saw police use in the park, and he spoke only when spoken to. She liked the corporal—it was the only name she knew him by—and felt safe with him.

The company of infantry whose mission was to keep the insurgents from returning to the devastated city, was set up in a temporary camp. They'd been without any amenities since the onslaught, and could hardly wait for the set to be hooked up. A bunch of them, eager to show off home-made movies, scrambled to connect their personal video cameras to the big screen. A staff sergeant restored order. They'd do it like the Academy Awards: there would be three categories: goriest, scariest, funniest. The winners, determined by audience reaction, would get to pick a souvenir of the Falouja engagement, from a cardboard container alongside the screen.

The films showed the soldiers breaking into houses, spraying lead at everything in sight. There were close-ups of dead bodies, of severed arms and legs, of eyes that seemed surprised to be out of their sockets. Edited in camera, MTV style, they ran about three minutes each, and would be shown proudly to family and friends when they got home.

The winner for 'funniest,' a sergeant, showed women caught in compromising positions. The sergeant was blindfolded, his hand positioned above the black box like the toy crane in amusement park grab-bags. He plunged it in and drew out his prize: a severed finger encrusted in blood. The audience whooped and hollered.

It was hot as hell, and they rolled the windows down. Caught up in private thoughts, trying to sort out doubts, regrets, anger, sadness, they didn't speak until Falouja was out of sight. The corporal shook his head back and forth.

"Treat these people worse than niggers," he said quietly.

"Why do you use that word?"

"It's all right if we do."

"I had my hand on my sidearm. I wanted to kill that sergeant."

"One man in a lynch mob's no worse'n the others. Don't matter who strings up the body."

"This mob wears uniforms." Maria said, thinking aloud. "They masquerade as heroes. Those of us who believed what we were told when we signed up . . . we've been fucked."

It was eerily quiet as they drove past one abandoned farm after another. Fields pockmarked with shell holes, were silent witness to the recent assault. Suddenly she stopped the Humvee.

"Hear that? Sounds like a dog . . . whining. It may be hurt."

She opened the door and stepped out.

"Bad idea, girl. It'll blow up in your face."

"It won't. I know it won't."

It was on the other side of the road. She walked over to it and bent down. It was a puppy. A boy puppy. It's coat was the color of the desert, except for a slash of black that ran across the face. It's eyes were closed but it trembled and whined.

"It's all right, it's all right," she whispered to the animal. "You're having a bad dream."

"Maria! Don't touch it!" The corporal was out of the Humvee, but he stayed across the road.

The puppy opened his eyes. The streak of black made it look like it was winking at her.

"I'm going to touch you. Don't be frightened."

"Maria!" the corporal begged.

She stroked the puppy's head, then his body. He stopped whining.

"What in hell you plannin' on doin' with it?"

They were back in the Humvee, the puppy on the seat between them.

"He must be hungry. I'm going to get him some milk. Cereal ought to be good too, don't you think?"

"I think you're crazy. Can't be no dog in the barracks." After a moment: "It's got some hound in him. Piece of meat would be better."

"We got plenty of Spam."

"They won't let you keep him."

"I'm keeping him until he's big enough to take care of himself."

The puppy started to bark.

"Maybe he's gotta go." She pulled over to the side of the road. "Bring my camera, will you?"

She put the puppy gently on the ground; he just looked up at her.

"Guess not." She picked him up and held him in her arms. "I'd like to remember him."

The corporal took a shot just as the puppy licked her face.

"That's love, man."

"I'd like one with you," Maria said. She handed the puppy to him, set the camera on the hood of the Hummer, and started the timer. The corporal held the dog up between them, and the shutter clicked.

As soon as they were on their way again, the puppy fell sound asleep on the corporal's lap.

"He needs a name."

Maria thought a minute: "'Hero' all right with you?"

The corporal nodded: "Learn him not to bark. Don't nobody have to know."

They looked at one another and smiled.

6

Los Angeles Times, March 27, 2005
Military Deaths

The Defense Department last week identified the following American military personnel killed in Iraq:

JONATHAN A. HUGHES, 21, of Lebanon, Ky.; specialist. Army National Guard. Hughes was killed March 19 when his Humvee struck a roadside bomb while he accompanied a U.S. convoy headed to Baghdad's airport. He was assigned to the 1st Battalion, 623rd Field Artillery Regiment, Army National Guard in Campbellsville, Ky.

LEE A. LEWIS JR., 28, of Norfolk, Va.; private first class. Army. Lewis was killed March 18 when his patrol was attacked with small-arms fire in the Sadr City section of Baghdad. He was assigned to the 3rd Battalion, 15th Infantry Regiment, 3rd Infantry Division at Fr. Stewart, Ga.

KEVIN S. SMITH, 20, of Springfield, Ohio; lance corporal, Marine Corps. Smith was killed Monday in enemy action in Al Anbar province. He was assigned to the 3rd Battalion, 2nd Marine Division, 2nd Marine Expeditionary Force at Camp Lejeune, NC

STEPHEN WILLIAMS, 23, of Biloxi, Mississippi, Corporal, Army. Williams was killed March 19 when checkpoint guards outside the city of Ramadi, mistook the supply truck he was in for an enemy vehicle, and sprayed it with machine gun fire. He was assigned to the 2nd Squadron, 278th Regimental Combat Team, Army National Guard in Biloxi, Mississippi.

MARIA SANCHEZ, 18, of Los Angeles, Cal.; private. Army. Sanchez, the driver, was killed March 19, in the same incident. She was assigned to the 4th Quartermaster Corps, 3rd Infantry Division, Fort Ord, Cal.

Maria's poetry was adapted from poems by Maya Cortes.

EDWARD LEWIS produced twenty-six feature films that garnered twenty-one Academy Awards and Nominations, eleven Golden Globes, the Palm d'Or at the Cannes Film Festival, and a British Film Academy Award. Among the films are *Spartacus*, *The River*, *Missing*, *Seconds*, *Grand Prix*, *The Fixer*, *Seven Days in May*, *Lonely are the Brave*, *The Iceman Cometh*, *Rhinoceros*, and *Lost in the Stars*.

He was the Co-Executive Producer of *The Thorn Birds* which won four Emmy Awards, and produced the original production on Broadway of *One Flew Over the Cuckoo's Nest*.

He received a Golden Globe Award for Best Producer of the Year, and a Screen Producers Guild Award as Best Producer of the Year.

He co-wrote two produced screenplays, *Spring Street*, a play produced Off Broadway, *The Good Life*, a musical produced at the Dynarsky Theatre in Hollywood, and *Ring-a-Ring-of-Rosy*, selected for The Harold Prince Musical Theatre Program.

Edward Lewis previous fiction includes the novel Heads You Lose, which he wrote in collaboration with his wife, Mildred Lewis.